"Okay, so you updated Miss Geist's wardrobe and found her a love slave, but what have you two done lately?" Amber harshly reminded me and De.

"Ours is a talent that does not expire, Amber," I said. "Unlike some people's grievous hairstyles."

"If I had a glove," the big-haired one responded petulantly, "I'd like totally toss down the gauntlet and challenge you to, let's see, revamp and romantically hook up some desperately needy nerd like—" Her brow furrowed in faux concentration. "Like . . . Ms. Leslie!"

"As if." Murray dismissed the possibility. "No way could Cher and De convert Miss Geist's girl to Bettydom, let alone find her a doable date."

"But if we can," De said sweetly, all up in Murray's face, "then you'll take me to the Whitney Houston film festival, right?"

"And if you can't," Murray said to De, throwing her a cocky, orthodontically correct smile, "then you go to the Forum with me for six action-packed hours of nonstop Wrestlemania!"

De glanced at me. "Piece of low-cal cake," I assured her.

Clueless™ Books

CLUELESS™ • A novel by H. B. Gilmour based on the film written and directed by Amy Heckerling

CHER'S GUIDE TO . . . WHATEVER • H. B. Gilmour

CHER NEGOTIATES NEW YORK • Jennifer Baker

AN AMERICAN BETTY IN PARIS • Randi Reisfeld

ACHIEVING PERSONAL PERFECTION • H. B. Gilmour

CHER'S FURIOUSLY FIT WORKOUT • Randi Reisfeld

FRIEND OR FAUX • H. B. Gilmour

CHER GOES ENVIRO-MENTAL • Randi Reisfeld

BALDWIN FROM ANOTHER PLANET • H. B. Gilmour

TOO HOTTIE TO HANDLE • Randi Reisfeld

CHER AND CHER ALIKE • H. B. Gilmour

TRUE BLUE HAWAII • Randi Reisfeld

ROMANTICALLY CORRECT • H. B. Gilmour

A TOTALLY CHER AFFAIR • H. B. Gilmour

Available from ARCHWAY Paperbacks

CLUELESS™

A Totally Cher Affair

H.B. Gilmour

AN ARCHWAY PAPERBACK
Published by POCKET BOOKS
New York London Toronto Sydney Tokyo Singapore

AN ARCHWAY PAPERBACK *Original*

An Archway Paperback published by
POCKET BOOKS, a division of Simon & Schuster Inc.
1230 Avenue of the Americas, New York, NY 10020

™ and Copyright © 1998 by Paramount Pictures

ISBN: 0-671-01905-8

First Archway Paperback printing February 1998

10 9 8 7 6 5 4 3 2 1

AN ARCHWAY PAPERBACK and colophon are registered trademarks of Simon & Schuster Inc.

Printed in the U.S.A.

IL: 7+

With gratitude to Donna Jerex, Associate Planner for the City of Santa Monica; the true blue Clueless trio of Randi, Anne, and Amira; and, as always, for John and Jessi, with love.

A Totally Cher Affair

Chapter 1

Charity is so fresh. My best friend, Dionne, and I are totally into doing good for humanity. Like making it more attractive. While others concentrate on saving the earth, De and I focus on actual people. We're like especially excellent at enhancing the looks and lives of our ensembly challenged, romantically impaired peers. We help our less fortunate classmates by any means necessary, giving of ourselves till it hurts.

As furious do-gooders, De and I get to attend the most frantic charity fiestas in our area, which is the way desirable Beverly Hills sector of Los Angeles. This opulent yet generous community is totally crawling with celebrities. My own father, Mel Horowitz, is one of them.

Daddy is a fully prominent attorney. He's a litigator, which is like the most vicious kind of lawyer. *People* magazine once called him the pit bull of the appellate court, so then everyone in my class was all, "Oh, Cher, your father is so cold." Not even. It's Daddy's job to be ruthless. In real life he's a total pussycat. So, anyway, we get invited to all the best benefit bashes. And De and I had spent Saturday evening at one of the most fun ever.

The festive fund-raiser was held at this media mogul's humongously sprawling estate. It so kicked. The sole disappointment of the evening was that Daddy's favorite movie star, Veronica Vidal, was a no-show. Veronica, for those who live in the popcorn-deprived Amazon basin, is like the last of the legendary screen goddesses. She's this golden mega-babe, the towering Uma of her day, with like Kate Hepburn's feisty elegance, Ann-Margret's chummy warmth, and Elizabeth Taylor's bad taste in men. She's been married eight times but is currently between spouses. Daddy was practically postal at the thought of meeting her. But the celebrated Hollywood hottie sent regrets.

The glittering bash turned out to be way Gen X, anyway. It was like Offspring of the Stars night or something. I mean, the band was all Jakob Dylan, and then Chastity Bono gave this fiery talk, and everyone was wearing Stella McCartney. Plus the food was cutting-edge excellent, both low-cal and free-range. There was this monster tent set up behind the tennis courts, and the pool was covered and converted into a wicked dance floor. And they had the best gifts. Each charitable attendee received a petite shopping bag seriously stuffed with sundry valuables.

"Did you totally love that heart charm that came in the goodie bag?" De asked. It was Sunday evening. Preparing for the school week at our respective casas, my true blue bud and I were telephonically reliving the gala.

Seated at my dressing table in my pink terry robe, freshly shampooed hair all twirled in a thick towel, I was trying out the ginseng astringent toner that had been tucked in our totes—along with a bounty of other state-of-the-art cosmetics, a discount coupon for a skin peel at Cedars of Santa Monica Hospital, and the fabulous little heart. "Totally," I agreed, dewy cheeks tingling with toner. "I am so wearing it with pride tomorrow."

"As if," my big complained. "Hello, I was going to wear mine."

"And?" I paused to ask.

"And I am so not into a Mary-Kate-and-Ashley thing, Cher."

While Dionne and I are nearly identical in many important ways—popularity, proven attractiveness, shopping skills—we are way not twins. I mean, I am all blond highlights, azure eyes, and it's like sunblock city if I don't want my pale skin to brutally blotch. De's eyes are a captivating hazel, her skin is the hue of a proper cappuccino, while her locks range from classic black to warm auburn, depending on her rinse and extension choices.

"I think our intimate friends will be able to tell us apart, Dionne," I pointed out. "And anyway, sporting dual charms tomorrow just says we attended the same awesomely desirable hunger benefit. I mean, probably Jakob and Chastity and Stella will be wearing theirs."

"Hunger?" said my homey. "Not even. Hello, how is life on planet Wrong?"

I was about to take exception to De's tone when she added, "Whoops, there's my other line. Hang on, okay? It's probably Murray."

Murray is Dionne's love interest, debate partner, and perpetual improvement project. Your typical loud-laughing, five-slapping, baggy-pants-and-funky-hat-wearing, immature male, he is De's primary boy-toy. That's boy as in high school boy, as opposed to man as in college or any other kind of real man. And toy as in, for De he's like this tall, cute, Ken doll she can cuddle, dress up, and scold. Bickering is one of the foundations of their relationship. And no one can do Angela Bassett's triumphant Tina to Lawrence Fishburne's defeated Ike like De proving a point to Murray.

As far as I'm concerned, high school is this vast wasteland when it comes to meeting quality guys. It's a total bonehead farm. On the other hand, it offers a wide variety of washouts with whom you can practice dating techniques. As high school boys go, Murray is among the most doable. And anyway, De is fully crushed on him.

"That was my boo," she confirmed, back on the line. "Guys are such trolls. He's all psyched over this random wrestling match at the Forum, featuring his fave hulk, Butta Boy. And the event falls on exactly the same day the cineplex is having their major Whitney Houston retrospective."

"Boys are so not into classical entertainment. But, De, you've got the complete Whitney collection on video, every movie she ever made," I tried to console her. "I mean, what is that, like four films?"

"It's not the same," my bud sighed.

"Bummer," I agreed. "Still, wasn't that fund-raiser the total bomb?"

"Wrestling so frosts me. Plus Butta Boy is singularly gross," my bud continued. "He weighs about two thousand pounds, and he's got so many stretch marks his skin looks like corduroy. Anyway, it wasn't hunger," De said. "It was the foremost killer, heart disease. They always have outstanding benders and the best bands."

"Dionne, last night's extravaganza was for ending hunger."

"Oh, really?" she challenged. "Then why was the charm shaped like a heart instead of like goat cheese or asparagus?"

"Duh," I begged to differ. "The hearts were thematic. They stand for Have a Heart, the evening's motto."

"How sure are you?"

"Only very. But I'll check with Daddy, okay?"

"Okay," De agreed. "Now, give me your honest opinion. I'm thinking either my Fendi midriff top with little sailorish Cap d'Antibes navy pants for tomorrow, or the tangerine silk chiffon Betsey Johnson cardigan with my beaded Anna Sui handkerchief hemline skirt."

"Mondays can be so bleak. I'd opt for fun. Go the Johnson-Sui route," I advised.

After disconnecting from De, I rough-dried my hair and schpritzed it with mint conditioning mousse to keep the frizzies at bay. Then, swathed in pink terry cloth, I padded down our sweeping marble staircase, heading for Daddy's study.

"Hi, Ma. What's happening?" I paused in our skylighted, domed entryway to address the ornately framed life-size portrait of my mom. She died in a heinous cosmetic mishap when I was just a baby. A lipo procedure gone wrong, they say. I like to think she still watches over me, so I update her sporadically.

"Daddy and I hit this awesome blowout yesterday, the primo event of the do-good circuit," I was saying, when I heard Daddy's voice raised in heated discussion. "It was a righteous fund-raiser for like this extremely worthy cause," I continued over the ruckus. "I think it was hunger, but De says heart disease. Anyway, you would have been proud of me, Ma. I was loqued out in this raging Azzedine Alaïa. Daddy wore the power Armani I picked out for him. The bash was rife with celebs, and we were total standouts."

At first I'd thought Daddy was on the phone, intimidating a prosecutor or something. But as I wrapped up the Mom bulletin, I recognized another voice coming from the study, the dulcet whine of my enviro-nerd former stepbrother, Josh. Josh, who's a couple of years older than me, is Daddy's ex-wife Gail's son by her second marriage. So we were legally related for like a big forty-five days, the total term of our parents' rash relationship.

It was apparently enough time for Josh and Daddy to furiously bond. And for Josh to develop the brutally mistaken notion that I needed his support and guidance. Ultimately, Gail and Josh returned to Seattle, where he fell into bad habits, like listening to mellow jazz, getting bent over ecological issues, and viewing fashion as a felony offense. Now, like the Terminator's threat, he was baack—attending UCLA and freeloading at our maisonette at whim.

I scuffed barefootedly to the study door and peeked in. Josh was holding a newspaper, whacking it with his hand, and going, "I can't believe you'd associate yourself with this kind of thing."

From behind his lawyerly mahogany desk, Daddy was scowling up at him impatiently.

There was a third party in the room. A rangy, rugged-looking guy, whose intense green eyes were framed by wire-rimmed granny glasses, was hunkered in Daddy's leather Eames chair, shaking his head. Said head was topped by a mass of chaotic sandy curls in brutal need of styling. A couple of years older than Josh, but way younger than Daddy, the unknown babe was sitting the way Abe Lincoln sits at the Lincoln Memorial, big-boned hands resting on his knees, a benevolent smile on his craggy face.

Josh and the mystery man seemed to share a garmental disability. Both were in basic lumberjack attire: jeans, work boots, and T-shirts. The craggy stranger at least had a rumpled bush jacket over his black tee. Josh's concession to style was the flannel shirt knotted around his waist.

"Give me that," Daddy shouted, standing abruptly. Josh deposited the newspaper into his outstretched hand. But instead of perusing the periodical, Daddy crumpled it up and tossed it viciously toward the brushed steel wastebasket. It hit the rim with this dull thud and plopped to the floor

"Swish," said the smiling stranger.

Daddy's big, jowly face swung toward him, glowering.

"Sorry," the guy said, still smiling.

He*llo*, what was going on here? Although Daddy and Josh have widely differing debate styles, they rarely engage in harsh exchanges. Josh is always respectful. Daddy is usually affectionately indulgent of the stepburden's politics, which, like Hush Puppies, are trendy yet antique. But everyone, except the bush-jacket babe, appeared to be way on the verge.

Realizing that I was in a bathrobe, makeup-less, my hair bitterly thirsting for volumizer, I hesitated at the door. But it looked like Daddy was heading for a blood pressure crisis, and I had to intervene. Anyway, my terry-cloth robe was a flattering pink hue, classically plush and cute, and Sergio had just colored me, so my drying locks were shimmering with highlights, and I'd done a beauty day at Arden, so my bare feet were wickedly pedicured. "Hi, everyone," I called from the door. "Josh, what a surprise. Don't tell me it's dinner time."

"Hey, Cher," the faux bro greeted me. "Still contributing to society via the sales tax?"

"That is such a ripe retort." I rolled my choice baby blue eyes. "Duh, hello. Everyone knows that spending stimulates the economy."

"She's right," the mystery man interjected with a laugh.

"Ruark, this is my little sister, Cher," Josh said.

"Little sister?" I tossed back my moist locks and fought the urge to hurl. "Not even," I objected. "We are so entirely not related."

"Come on, you kids, make nice," Daddy said, plainly relieved to see me.

"Cher, this is Ruark Rosner," Josh introduced the curly-haired Lincolnesque intruder, who unfurled from the chair to greet me. "Nice to meet you," he said, the green gaze behind his John Lennon specs kind of sparkly with fun. "Well, Josh, Mel, I guess we're kind of finished here, right? I should probably go."

"Yeah, yeah." Daddy gave the guy a tight smile. "Go." He waved a hand dismissively at Ruark. "I'll think about what you said."

"Can't ask for more than that. I know the way out. Thanks for your time." With a nod, Josh's friend departed.

The minute he was gone, Daddy starting shaking his finger at Josh. "You're wrong. I said I'd listen. I listened. I'll think about it like I promised that guy. But you're wrong."

"Thanks for seeing him, Mel. You just need—"

"Stop!" Daddy held up his hand like a traffic cop, fully silencing Josh. "I know what I need. Don't tell me what I need. You know what I need? I need a corned beef on rye. Right now." Daddy started for the door.

Corned beef, this lipid-drenched slab of ethnic cleansing, was one of the major no-nos on Daddy's low-fat, low-cholesterol diet. "Hel*lo*," I sang out. "You can't have corned beef."

Daddy whirled toward me, all red-faced and upset. "I can't *what?*" he demanded.

"Have corned beef," I repeated cheerfully.

Volcanically steamed, Daddy lowered his head and peered grimly at me over the rims of his reading glasses.

"Er, without like celery tonic or cream soda to go with it, right?" I added, blinking innocently up at him.

He patted my head. "That's a great idea. I'm going to run down to Canter's and pick up a couple of bottles."

"Daddy, wait," I said.

"What is it now?" he growled.

"It's just a question. I mean, you know more about this than I do," I began.

"More about what?" Daddy cut me off impatiently.

"Heart disease or hunger," I started to explain. "De says—"

"I am not making a choice between heart disease and hunger, Cher. I'm just getting myself a lousy corned beef sandwich!" Daddy hollered. "And I'm not going to discuss this any further."

"No, Daddy. I mean that benefit we were at last night. What was it for?"

Josh gave this lame snort and went like, "I don't believe it. You don't even know which organization you were supporting?"

"Excuse me, may I see your ticket to this discussion? Whoops. No ticket. I guess you weren't invited to participate in my private conversation, Josh, were you?" I turned back to Daddy, who was heading for the door. "It was about hunger, right?"

"Either that or whales," Daddy said. "No, it was hunger. I'm totally for ending hunger. In fact, that's what I'm going to do right now."

"I can't believe you didn't know the cause you were supposed to be championing," Josh said again as Daddy left. "And what was that celery tonic thing? You totally wussed on the forbidden corned beef issue."

"As if," I responded. "It was a question of priorities. Would it have been better to argue Daddy into cardiac arrest than allow him a few grams of saturated fat? Duh, I don't think so. And if you're so concerned with his health, why didn't you try to do something?"

"Get between Mel and a deli sandwich? No thanks," my former stepnightmare conceded with a sheepish smile. "I'm sorry I got him all cranked up like that. I just thought he needed more information, so I called Ruark." Josh shrugged, then changed the subject. "So, last night's fund-raiser a success?"

"Outstanding," I conceded. "The Wallflowers did this stompin' set. Jakob Dylan was a raw visual treat and so poetic, all garbed in nerd chic—you know, dark jacket, shirt collar all buttoned up. And Chastity was wearing this fresh Stella McCartney frock with like these amazing ornaments by Alexander McQueen, the bad boy of Brit couture—"

As I spoke, Josh's smile faded. He shook his head. "Is that all you got out of attending the benefit—who was wearing what?"

I refused to let the UCLA Boy Scout pin a guilt badge on me. "Excuse me. There was so much more," I countered. "The cuisine, the gift bags, the fabulously famous guests, although Veronica Vidal, who was listed as one of the event's most glittering sponsors, never showed. But enough about my bustling life. Who's this Ruark guy anyway? I mean, what kind of information was he supposed to deliver to Daddy?"

"It wouldn't interest you," Josh said. "Anyway, I've got to split."

"You're leaving? Why? Did we run out of food?" I asked sarcastically.

With this dramatic, exasperated sigh, Josh shook his head at me, then turned on his shabby work boots and bailed.

I was so not crushed, but way curious. What was going on? Why had a rumpus erupted between Josh and Daddy? And what, as Tina Turner might've asked, did the wire-rimmed babe in the bush jacket have to do with it? So the moment the front door locked behind Josh, automatically resetting our chronic security system, I rushed to retrieve the crumpled newspaper Daddy had angrily tried to fling into the trash.

But there was no clue in the paper, not on the page Josh had gotten all worked up over. Totally nothing of interest, not even like an ad for a decent shoe sale or designer personal appearance. There was nothing but this boring photograph of an ancient L.A. hacienda, about which some dull civic feud was raging.

Chapter 2

*T*he next morning in social studies, my
best bud, looking way choice in her Betsey J. crop-top
and funky Sui skirt, uttered seven of my favorite
words: "You were right, I was wrong, Cher."

Sitting side by side in Miss Geist's room, accepting
compliments on our attire from passing fans, De and
I were still discussing Saturday's excellent bender. "It
was a benefit for hunger. How could I have doubted
you?" she continued as I mouthed, "Thank you," to a
group of our classmates who had paused to applaud
our garmental choices.

I had selected a killer lavender leather minifrock to
keep the Monday blues at bay. And De and I were
both wearing our golden goodie-bag hearts. Looking
adorably Victorian, mine dangled from a velvet neck
ribbon, while De had threaded hers through the gold

hoop of her navel ring. "It's an understandable mistake," I said generously. "The bash was so fun it could've been heart disease."

A paper airplane hit the back of my head, lodging in my lustrous follicles. Annoyed, I pulled the craft out of my hair. It had De's name scrawled on the fuselage. "For you," I said, handing it over. "Let me guess, could it be from your main boo? Why can't the boy use a Touch-Tone like everyone else?"

Actually, at that very moment, half the class was cellularly conversing with their support personnel: friends, trainers, aromatherapists, financial planners, whatever. Others surfed the Net on their laptops or leafed through teen 'zines of choice. Like Nobushi was all slack-jawed over *Thrasher,* the boardies' bible, while, fooling practically no one, Brittany was browsing her subscription copy of *Tiger Beat,* which she had hidden inside a back issue of French *Vogue.*

Across the aisle, Jesse Fiegenhut, whose father is a major player in the music business, was sampling new CDs. Tiffany Gelfin was hot-rolling Tiffany Fukashima's hair, while Shawana braided the long, blond-streaked locks of Nathan Kahakalau, our transfer student from Kalani High in Honolulu—a ragin' Keanu and heir to a pineapple fortune.

The sole oasis of calm in our otherwise tumultuous classroom was the desk at which our social studies instructor, Miss Geist, was polishing off a breakfast croissant and going over the attendance book with her new teaching assistant, Ms. Leslie.

Hearsay had it that the drab twenty-something

was an education major from Chicago who had recently transferred to the greater Los Angeles area. Part of her training apparently involved a six-week stint at our school. With her oversize glasses, lackluster hair, and shapeless costumes in overpowering floral prints, the teacher-in-training was not only aiding Miss Geist, she was practically her clone.

Actually, Ms. Leslie looked more like Miss Geist than Miss Geist did since De and I had worked our makeover magic on our formerly clueless social studies teacher.

I studied the educational duo while De read the missile from Murray. Croissant crumbs littered Miss Geist's dark blouse. A smudge of scarlet lipstick tainted her smile. Still, the teacher had come a long way since Dionne and I did her color chart and introduced her to the twin miracles of moisturizing lotion and volumizer mousse. And masterminded her romance with Mr. Hall, our favorite English meister, to whom Miss Geist was now blissfully married.

De folded up the note. "It's from Mr. Maturity," she confirmed. "He's formally inviting me to the Butta Boy vs. Mongo gala."

"Mongo?" I said.

"This shaved-head, pasty-white behemoth who is, if possible, even more grotesque than Butta Boy," De advised.

Rolling our eyes, we both turned in Murray's direction. De's Nautica-clad honey and his Hilfiger-bedecked homey, Sean, were two rows behind us, grunting and growling and menacing each other with action figures. Murray had a rubbery multi-headed Venom in one hand and a G.I. Joe in the other, while Sean brandished a pair of winged Dragon Flyz.

"They're playing with dolls," I said.

"Pathetic," De murmured. She caught Murray's eye and tapped the airborne invitation. "No way am I giving up a Whitney retrospective to witness the battle of the blubber," she informed him.

Two of our true blues, Tai and Baez, and one of our irritants, Amber, straggled into class as the bell tolled.

"Excellent Monday choices," said Tai, whose plain brown hair was highlighted with a dazzling blue streak. She gave us a thumbs-up sign. "De, that handkerchief hem is so Winona. Ooo, and Cher, I love that pastel leather."

"Well, I'm like totally opposed to it." This surprising comment came from Tai's occasional companion, the eminent slacker fashion critic, Ryder Hubbard. "I mean, how rare are purple cows anyway?" the boy with room-temperature IQ asked, tossing back his lank, shoulder-length locks with a jerk of his head. "And like if even one was slaughtered to make that dress, whoa, dudes, what a cosmic crime against nature."

Even Tai, who normally hung on Ryder's every weird pronouncement, was taken aback by this passionate outburst. She took the boy's hand—the one in which the homework he'd just purchased from Ringo Farbstein was clutched, not the one gripping his decal-ridden skateboard—and patted it soothingly.

"Don't mind Ryder," our pal Baez, of the severely peroxided buzz cut, said. "As one of a kind, he's like brutally bonded with endangered species."

"Well, I'm opposed to leather, too." Amber crashed the conversation. The girl whom fashion forgot was wearing one of her vintage ensembles. It was supposed to be this "Swinging London" look, complete with white lipstick, big hair, and this geometric fringe of bangs that looked like it had been laminated into place. But in her shiny white go-go boots and boldly patterned plastic shift, she looked like a Spice Girl in a shower curtain. "As an ecologically concerned consumer," our childhood bane declared, "I'm through with animal products. Leather, fur, wool, alpaca—"

"So you're saying what?" Shawana asked. "That vinyl is the fabric of our lives?"

"Wake up and smell the henna, Amber. Bouffants are over," I gently advised.

"And bangs blow," De added.

Miss Geist stood up. "All right, class." She clapped her slender hands. The golden glint of her simple wedding band warmed me as always. De and I had placed that ring on her finger as surely as Mr. Hall had, only way more symbolically, of course. Miss Geist noticed my smile and returned it. Then she got all flustered as I pointed to the croissant flakes dotting her blouse and signaled for her to wipe the lipstick off her teeth.

"Speaking of over," Amber mumbled beside me, "someone tell Ms. Leslie that farmyard frock she's wearing went out with Lassie's mom. The woman's taste buds are heinously impaired."

Much as I enjoy disagreeing with the Am-burden, in this instance, I couldn't. Ms. Leslie did appear to be garmentally challenged, big time. Maybe even more ensembly impaired than Miss Geist had been before De and I overhauled her.

"All right, class. While Ms. Leslie returns the compositions you handed in last week, I'd like to discuss an item in the news," Miss Geist was saying, "an issue everyone in our city is concerned about."

"Oh, no, not the Gwyneth Paltrow–Brad Pitt affair again," Tai groaned.

"She said news, Tai, not history," Amber hissed. Snatching her essay from Ms. Leslie's hand, the disco-haired one glanced at the paper. "Hello, excuse me. What is this?" she demanded.

"Why, that looks exactly like your composition, Amber," De said, craning her slender neck to study the report. "But someone put a great big D across the top of it."

"Did anyone see the piece on the Llewellyn mansion in yesterday's *Times?*" Miss Geist asked.

Amber's hand flew up.

"Yes, Amber?" Miss Geist seemed delighted. "You read the newspaper article yesterday?"

"Hello, did I have time to read, Miss Geist? Oh, sure, on the day of my first lymphatic drainage massage at Skin Ease? I think not. I was totally releasing toxins yesterday. So, whoops, excuse me for not steeping myself in CNN." Miss Geist stood there for a moment, her smile stiff, her owlish glasses sliding down her nose, trying to understand what Amber's facial had to do with the Llewellyn estate. Finally she went, "Then you didn't read the *Times* article?"

"The *Times* is not the paper in question," Amber snapped. The *Times* did not get a D, did it? No, this"—she waved her report—"is the paper I'm concerned with."

Miss Geist caught her assistant's eye, and Ms. Leslie, after shrugging innocently, turned to Amber. "The assignment was a two-page essay on disaster relief, Amber," the TA gently explained, "and you submitted a list of hairdressers who make house calls in the Beverly Hills area."

"And?" Amber demanded.

"Well, what do hairdressers have to do with getting aid to flood victims in the midwest?" Ms. Leslie asked.

"Hello. You said disaster relief, you didn't say floods," Amber said, dismissing both the question and Ms. Leslie. "And anyway, Miss Geist," she continued pointedly, "all last week I was like in anticipatory angst over my lymphatic session, which is why I couldn't focus on your little extra-credit essay. But I did my best, which so deserves more than a D."

"Sit down, Amber. Did anyone see yesterday's paper?" Miss Geist asked desperately.

My heart went out to her. I stood. "If you mean that little front-page item on Ronald Blunt, the self-promoting gazillionaire real estate developer getting

20

ready to tear down this old L.A. hacienda in order to build a crucial new five-acre shopping complex, yes, Miss Geist, I did happen to glance at the piece."

"Ronald Blunt, whose daughter, Kiki, is modeling's total flavor of the month," De asked, "with like two big fashion shows and a teen 'zine cover to her credit?"

"She's a hoochie mama," said Nathan, flexing his right hand, which was sheathed in a fingerless leather driving glove.

"I hear you, bro," Murray agreed, and he and Sean leaped up and slapped the Hawaiian Lion five.

"Hoochie mama?" Shawana asked.

"High heels, tight jeans, bandeau tops," I translated for her, proving that the field trip De and I had recently masterminded to true blue Hawaii had been way educational.

"Excuse me, did someone say new five-acre shopping complex?" Baez demanded.

"The Llewellyn mansion is one of Los Angeles' most treasured landmarks," Miss Geist was saying in this impassioned voice. "It's inconceivable that it be destroyed to make way for yet another—"

"Mall!" The two Tiffanys shouted together. And suddenly, the whole class was like, "Yess! How awesome is that? A new shopping op in the neighb'. A total consumer theme park. How brutally excellent!"

You could tell Miss Geist was disappointed. "All right, everyone. Attention. Hello. People!" She futilely tried to call the class to order.

Suddenly Ms. Leslie put two fingers to her lips and released this ear-splitting whistle. It was furiously effective. Everyone went all silent and like gaped at the teaching assistant. Miss Geist's eyebrows, which De and I had personally shaped, flew up in astonishment. "Er, thank you, Maura," she said to Ms. Leslie.

"Maura?" De whispered to me.

"Maura Leslie," I responded. "Acceptable name. Wicked whistle."

"Now, class." Miss Geist was blinking earnestly behind her big glasses. "I want you to find yesterday's article. Use the library or your computers— but I expect you to find and read the *Times* piece. Because tomorrow we're going to have a visitor who will be addressing this topic. The destruction of historic buildings is an important civic issue. And your assignment is to be prepared to listen and participate intelligently in tomorrow's discussion and, hopefully, in the preservation of your community."

"Miss Geist was way fiery today," De remarked as we left social studies.

"And classically attired, too," I added, autographing the Bisou-Bisou shopping bag an adoring ninth grader had thrust at me.

"Thanks to you," my bud acknowledged graciously. Borrowing my marbled Montblanc, she signed the grateful girl's bag, too, dotting the *i* in *Dionne* with her trademark heart.

"De, you were totally essential to Miss Geist's transformation. I could never have accomplished it without your support," I protested, tucking the returned pen back into my new Ungaro mint nylon minipurse.

"I do what I can," she said, over the din of Ryder's skateboard. Slaloming between students, Tai's fatal attraction executed this screeching wheelie, then crashed into the sophomore lockers. "But the Geist-Hall merger was one of your most blatantly inspired matches, Cher," De continued. "And while not exactly a full-out Betty, Miss Geist is no longer a lonely Monet."

"Except for the crumb spillage, she's looking way Michelle Pfeiffer in *Dangerous Minds*," I agreed.

"While Ms. Leslie is all Edward James Olmos in *Stand and Deliver*." Like a wave full of medical waste washing onto a Malibu beach, Amber had caught up with us. Murray, Sean, and Nathan were right behind her, the hems of their dragging baggy jeans rustling along the corridor Congoleum.

"Oooo, that was cold," Sean remarked.

"Word up, bro. Way harsh," Nathan agreed, slapping Sean's digits with his leather-gloved hand.

"Well, it's not as harsh as living in the past." Ambu-loser pouted, taking a tiny tape recorder from her purse. "Cher and De's remake of Miss Geist is beyond Jurassic," she said into the mini recorder. "It's like pitifully Pleistocene—"

Tai and Janet Hong joined us. "Jurassic is way older than Pleistocene," Janet commented mildly.

Amber shot her an evil squinchie. "Note," she addressed her petite recorder. "Find colorful synonyms for *old*. Like maybe *stale*."

"Amber, what are you doing?" Tai asked, looking at the tape recorder.

"Duh, I guess I'm talking to myself," the big-haired one replied sarcastically. "If you must know, I'm taking notes for this epic of teen angst I'm writing. It's called 'Frappuccino Nation.' It's about how we've sold out for franchised sweets."

"Amber in bangs gives new meaning to the phrase *lunatic fringe*," De confided to me.

"I mean, excuse me," Amber continued, tucking the recorder back into her purse. "Okay, so you updated Miss Geist's wardrobe and found her a love slave, but what have you two done lately?"

"Besides wearing out the video of *Waiting to Exhale?*" Murray asked. Beneath his backward golf cap, his dark eyes twinkled mischievously. And the meager lip fuzz of which he was so proud curled into this amused little grin.

De shot a hazel-eyed warning at the boy, while I focused my azure orbs on Amber, whose flamboyant follicles were this inflamed shade of red.

"Ours is a talent that does not expire, Amber," I said, "unlike some people's grievous hairstyles."

"If I had a glove," the go-go-booted one responded petulantly, "I'd throw it down now. I'd like totally toss down the gauntlet and challenge you—"

"Chall-*enge*. Chall-*enge*. Chall-*enge!*" the three stooges started chanting. Alana and Baez drifted over.

"Challenge us to what?" De demanded.

"Oh, I don't know," Amber drawled innocently, "to, let's see, revamp and romantically hook up some damaged dork, some desperately needy nerd like—" Her brow furrowed in faux concentration. Then, as other students began to move toward us, she snapped her acrylically enhanced fingertips. "Like . . . Ms. Leslie!" she gloated.

There was this collective gasp.

"Ms. Leslie from social studies?" Murray was taken aback.

"Ms. Leslie, whose drab brown hair is so randomly shorn it looks nibbled, not styled?" Alana asked.

"Ms. Leslie, who wears those Ozark Mountain off-the-racks and, excuse me, no makeup?" Baez gasped.

A crowd now surrounded us. "Hello, not even Moesha does no makeup," Shawana called out.

"Okay, Winona Ryder and Jodie Foster go bare-faced occasionally," our friend Summer said, joining the fray, "but one has great bones and the other a degree from Yale."

"Ms. Leslie." De considered the candidate.

"Maura," I said, recalling the ear-splitting blast with which the teaching assistant had silenced our class. There was something way spunky about that whistle, something chronic and unplugged. Deep inside the meek fashion innocent a vibrant spark of life longed to be released. I turned to De. She was smiling, too.

"That whistle," I said softly.

De nodded. "There's more to Maura than meets the eye."

"As if." Murray dismissed the possibility. "No way could you two convert Miss Geist's girl to Bettydom."

"Straight up," Sean agreed. "Only a miracle could turn her into a bona fide babe."

"Let alone find her a doable date," Murray insisted.

"But if we can," De said sweetly, all up in Murray's face, "then you'll take me to the Whitney Houston film festival, right?"

"Never happen. She's toast, man." Sean slapped Murray's navy and gold Nautica-draped back.

"And if you can't," Murray said to De, brightening now, throwing her a cocky, orthodontically correct smile, "then you go to the Forum with me for six action-packed hours of nonstop Wrestlemania!"

De's grin wavered briefly. She glanced at me. "Piece of low-cal cake," I assured her.

Suddenly, Nathan unsheathed his driving hand and slapped his glove into Amber's palm. "Do it, wahine mama," he urged. "Throw down the calfskin gauntlet. What's the challenge?"

"All right." Amber raised the glove in her clenched fist. "I defy Cher and De to transform Ms. Leslie from geek to goddess," she announced, "and snag her a blazing Baldwin of her own."

"By Saturday," Murray added.

"I was getting to that," Amber snapped. "By Saturday." Then, dramatically, forcefully, she threw down the glove. It landed on the prized and polished size-ten Nikes of Ms. Diemer, our humorless P.E. coach.

"Drop down and give me twenty," the gym teacher snarled.

"Get a life," Amber blurted.

Pumped at the prospect of bettering Ms. Leslie, I felt a burst of pity for the girl with the unmanageable mouth. "Whoops, we're late for English. Sorry, Ms. D.," I said. And grabbing Amber's arm, I rushed our rash t.b. into Mr. Hall's classroom.

Chapter 3

*S*hort, balding, and clothed in generic
teacher threads, Mr. Hall was chalking something
onto the blackboard as we entered. His aged tweed
jacket, trousers that bagged at the knee, faded blue
Oxford shirt, and clip-on paisley bow tie told the sad
story of how insupportive our society is of education.

"Ouch," Amber yelped belatedly. With a vicious
squeak of plastic, she wrested her arm from my
hand.

"That's 'thank you' in Amber-speak," De commented, sliding into her front-row seat.

"Oh, excuse me," retro girl grumbled, dramatically rubbing her arm. "Did I forget to express my
gratitude for the heinous bruise I'm probably going to
have?"

Baez brushed by us. "It's a good thing you keep a plastic surgeon on retainer, Amber," she said.

"Her plastic surgeon wears a retainer?" Tiffany G. asked.

"That is such a coincidence," mused Tiffany F. "Mine is having his teeth bleached, and he has to wear this gross mouthpiece."

The bell rang as I adjusted my lavender leather mini and slid into the seat behind De. Across the aisle from us, lips moving, Ryder was trying to read the list Mr. Hall had scrawled on the blackboard: "Dissident. Mandela. Sharansky. Wei Jingsheng."

"Dissident." Mr. Hall helped him, drawing a line under the first word. Everyone went *"Yeeww!"* at the icky sound of chalk scraping the board. Mr. Hall winced, too, then shrugged apologetically. "All right," he said, clearing his throat. "Does anyone know what *dissident* means?" Ringo's and Janet's hands went up a second before Mr. Hall finished his sentence with, "besides Ringo and Janet?"

There was this moment of stumped silence, during which the brainer couple withdrew their hands.

"Let's break the word down," Mr. Hall suggested. "Tai—"

Tai turned hopefully to Janet, but the gifted Betty had so moved on and was browsing a Sharper Image catalog. Tossing back her blue-streaked hair, Tai courageously plunged in. "Okay, so like *diss* is an insult. And *dent,* is that from the same root as dental? Like insulting teeth or something?"

Mr. Hall's mouth fell open. Amber went, "Break out the lunar module, Tai's lost in space again." But

Ryder started pounding his desk. "Let's hear it for the girl," he shouted encouragingly. "Nice try, dude, nice try."

"Insulting teeth," Mr. Hall mused. "Very, er . . . interesting. Thank you, Tai. No, actually, the root we're looking for is *dissent.* Can anyone use *dissent* in a sentence?"

"Oo, oo, me, me!" Elvis Romanov, this recent arrival from Russia, stood up, waving his hand.

"Yes?" Mr. Hall said, brightening.

"I shop de whole Armani section," Elvis proudly recited, "but I don't find a *dissent* suit."

You could tell right away the boy had blown it. I hated the way Mr. Hall was just standing there, blinking and shaking his head. He looked way discouraged. Compassion for the underpaid teacher drove me to my feet.

"Dissent," I began. Then I had to wait for everyone to quiet down. There were all these whistles and kids were applauding and calling out things like, "Cher, you have the totally best wardrobe," and "Lavender leather rules!"

I went, "Thank you. Thanks, people," and finally, as the outburst ended, I finished with, "Okay, so, dissent. Dissent is like disagreeing, right? Having another opinion."

"That's it," Mr. Hall broke in, with this relieved little smile. "Thank you, Cher. To *dissent* is to differ in sentiment or opinion. And a dissident is someone who dissents."

He tapped the blackboard again as I took my seat. "Here are three famous dissidents who have captured world attention. All of them have been imprisoned for advocating beliefs that were in conflict with the policies of their countries. Natan Sharansky, who protested human rights abuses in the Soviet Union. Nelson Mandela, jailed for twenty-seven years for demanding an end to apartheid in South Africa. And, finally, this man, Wei Jingsheng, whose writings and letters from prison are collected in this book."

Mr. Hall held up this volume called *The Courage to Stand Alone*. "Wei"—he pronounced it *Way*—"was sentenced to fifteen years in prison for writing and posting in a public place—a wall, actually, a kind of community bulletin board known as the Democracy Wall—a pamphlet calling for political freedom in China. After his release, when he continued to express his dissent in interviews and letters to the world press, he was arrested again and sentenced to an additional fourteen years."

"That is so harsh," Tai offered.

"Wei," Mr. Hall continued.

"You said it," Ryder passionately agreed.

Mr. Hall paused, stared at the fervent slacker, then said, "No, I meant, Wei, the man, not *way* the adverb."

"Whatever," Amber said, making the *W* sign and faking this grossly bored look. "And your point is?"

"Yes, well," Mr. Hall went on, "Wei's courage has also been documented in an award-winning film by Trudie Styler, called *A Voice for Chinese Democracy*."

"Trudie Styler?" Jesse switched off his CD player and plucked out his earphones. "Sting's babe?"

"Hello, Trudie is Sting's *wife*," De informed him.

"Really?" Mr. Hall acted all new.

"Definitely," said Alana, whose father, a national network news anchor, gets invited to all these slammin' MTV bashes. "Trudie is this prominent filmmaker. She lives a furiously independent life."

"If *I* were married to Sting, I'd like do nothing but look fabulous and follow him around," Tiffany F. reported, sighing.

Baez shook her peroxided head disapprovingly, which set off this wind-chime collision of earrings. The silver skull dangling from her right lobe clanged against her hanging minidice, Cartier hoops, and sterling leaf ear pendant by Erickson Beamon for Ghost. "You'd throw away your own life to be slavishly devoted to a world-class Baldwin?" she charged.

"Quit raggin' on the girl," Sean called out. "Tiffany, I totally respect your point of view. What're you doing Friday night?"

"Hel*lo!*" Amber, the instant-gratification queen, broke into the conversation again. "At the risk of being repetitious, people—whatever! Is this discussion leading somewhere?"

"Whoa, Amberina." Ryder held up his hands in surrender. "The dude just asked her for a date. He's not talking commitment yet."

"Oh, let me take a guess," Summer said sarcastically. "Could all this talk of freedom possibly be leading to what *every* discussion in this school leads to—homework?"

Her remark stung. A sudden, panicked silence fell. Pleading for denial, all eyes focused on Mr. Hall.

"Well, yes," he began sheepishly, to a chorus of outraged grumbles and groans. "But wait. Just listen to this." The earnest academic began leafing through *The Courage to Stand Alone.* "Although Wei's purpose is extremely serious and important, he often writes with humor, even sarcasm, to make his point. Here." Hall thumped a page. "After protesting students were murdered in Tiananmen Square, Wei wrote to Deng, the man responsible for his imprisonment and that vicious massacre: 'I've long known that you are precisely the kind of idiot to do something foolish like this, just as you've long known that I am precisely the kind of idiot who will remain stubborn to the end and take blows with his head up. . . . We have an intimate mutual disgust—'"

"Which is probably the best Sean and Tiffany could even hope for," Amber murmured.

But I did think the letter was pretty spunky for a guy who'd been in jail longer than I'd been alive. "Here's something else he wrote. 'Your problem,'" Mr. Hall continued quoting Wei's diss, "'is that you have too much ambition, too little talent, and you're narrow-minded.'" Our teacher skimmed his notes. "Here's another one Wei Jingsheng wrote to Deng," he announced. "Wei was very sick at the time. He'd been mistreated in prison, lost most of his teeth, and had been in isolation for so long that he could hardly speak. But when it was suggested that he change his position, retract his support for democracy, in exchange for medical treatment and leniency, he wrote: 'You think I can lie so lightly? If you want to be irresponsible, that's your problem. But I refuse to be that way. For the sake of the nation, I will follow my conscience.' "

After reading further selected highlights of the dissident's correspondence, including " 'The reason why America is ahead in everything is that Americans have free speech, even the freedom to say things that are wrong,' " Mr. Hall assigned the class to write its own letters defending a principle.

"You want us to defend the principal?" Nathan was perplexed.

"No, not *the* principal, a principle," Mr. Hall clarified, "a belief, an ideal, a viewpoint. Using some of Wei Jingsheng's letters as your example," he said, picking up this sheaf of papers from his desk and distributing them to us, "I want each of you to take a stand for or against a controversial and current issue. Something in the news. Something important to our community. Something you like that's being threatened or something you dislike and want changed. Then prepare persuasive letters to the authorities stating your views. And you can freely do this because in our country people are not sent to prison for expressing dissent."

De's hand was up. Her pale pink juliettes were frantically fluttering.

"Yes, Dionne?" Mr. Hall said, just as the bell rang and everyone started gathering their belongings. Cell phones were snapped shut. CD players were paused. Blow-dryers, laptops, Game Boys, and remote control minivehicles were switched off and put away. Hair accessories, makeup kits, blemish cremes, fashion 'zines, and framed photos of loved ones were tucked into baby blue, lime green, moss, ecru, and coral-hued backpacks.

"But, Mr. Hall," Dionne feebly protested over the deafening end-of-class chaos. "Our community is clean, opulent, landscaped, secure, and brutally brimming with the bounty of life. I am fully not trying to shirk my homework, but what's not to like in Beverly Hills?"

"De is so right," I supported my t.b.'s dissent. "Complaining is okay for the oppressed," I called, shouldering my fuzzy teddybear backpack and slipping my def silver compact of shimmering eye shadows by Hard Candy into my Ungaro minipurse. "But we, the people of Beverly Hills, so have nothing to protest."

"I totally agree with Dionne," Tai said fifteen minutes later, when we were assembled on the volleyball court for P.E.

Although Bronson Alcott High's gymsuits are one hundred percent preshrunk, prefaded, quality cotton, they come in only one color, basic black. So, of course, I and my t.b.'s took a furious pass on those bland uniforms. We were garbed instead in a neon rainbow of flattering designer sportswear. Unfortunately, we had to wear these gold or green sashes over our clothes. They were supposed to show which team you were on. Like we'd really forget if we didn't have a lame swatch of fabric to glance at. Anyway, I was glad my crew got to wear gold. Not just because it's, well, golden, but it's a way more neutral shade. Green clashes with practically everything.

Beneath her gold sash, Tai was mail-orderly clad in a Victoria's Secret silk-and-cotton blend crocheted tank top with raspberry rolled-hem shorts. "Mr. Hall's assignment thoroughly blows," she finished.

"I guess that's why they call it home *work*," said Amber, in floral spandex bike shorts and a sleeveless zip-front tunic, "instead of home *play*."

"Teachers just don't get it," Alana ventured, as an opposing team jockette spiked a ball over the net at us. "I mean, if you're against something, like heart disease, it would be pretty lame to sit around writing letters, like, 'Dear Mr. Cholesterol,' when you could just throw a frantic fund-raiser."

"Wouldn't it be fresh to chair a junior charity event?" I mused, adjusting my gold sash so that the sporty stripe on my Mossimo terry top showed. "To like raise money and consciousness about some righteous cause? That could be so excellent."

"Yesss!" In a spontaneous gesture of support, Baez raised her fist, accidentally punching the volleyball. It flew back over the net.

"Set it up, gold. Set it up!" Coach Diemer shouted. "This is a team sport."

"My dad and stepmom went to this trippin' bash

that either Iggy Pop or Ozzie Osborne hosted," Summer was saying. "And like Jewel wrote the theme song. Only I forgot the disease. Juvenile diabetes, I think."

"Hel*lo*, it couldn't have been juvenile anything," Amber protested. "Iggy and Ozzie are both grossly overaged. And Jewel is at least twenty-three."

"Maybe it was my mom and stepdad who went." Summer rethought the event. "But speaking of charity, De, can I see that charm you got at Saturday's fiesta?"

"It's just like Cher's," my partner in party-going said as the ball returned to our court. Lifting her peach mist Shaker knit sports sweater to show Janet the heart dangling from her navel ring, De's elevated elbow caught the ball, sending it in Amber's direction.

"Yeeuw, watch out for my nose!" the plastic princess shrieked, batting the sphere away.

Shawana, who had been bent over tying the striped laces of her Air Rebecca Lobo high-tops, straightened abruptly. The volleyball connected with her spine. Bouncing off the center strap of her kiwi spandex racerback, it sailed back over the net.

"Enough with the fancy stuff, gold team," Ms. Diemer yelled. "Hit it with your hands or you're disqualified."

"Hit what?" Alana wanted to know. "What is she buggin' about now?"

"Whatever!" Tiffany Gelfin made the W sign. The volleyball flew toward her, landing on her upraised forefingers and cracking two iridescent blue juliettes.

"Medic. School nurse. EMS!" Tiffany Fukashima screamed on her bud's behalf. "Anyone got nail glue?"

"We really could throw the cleanest do-good blast ever," I decided, getting pumped at the prospect. "All we need is a cause."

"Like what?" De asked me. "Everybody does disease and endangered species."

"Ms. Diemer, we have a lacerated acrylic here!" Tiffany F. was waving at the coach when some wiry stooge on the other side sent the ball hurtling at her. *"Ay-yeee!"* she screamed, defensively curling her vulnerable French-tip-topped fingers into fists. The descending globe hit her knuckles and arched skyward toward Tai.

"What is it with this ball?" our blue-streaked bud grumbled. "You can't even have a decent discussion without getting interrupted every five seconds." Annoyed, Tai jumped up and slammed the volleyball over the net. "And keep it over there," she hollered. "We're trying to plan a party!"

Ms. Diemer started blowing her shrill whistle. "Rotate!" she bellowed.

"That is so rude," Summer yelled back.

The whistle blasts were way severe, fully detrimental to our hearing. De stuck her fingers into her ears, then she went, "Eek! I think I punctured an eardrum. I told Yoshi these juliettes were too long."

"Rotate!" Diemer was making these frantic twirling gestures with her callused digits. "Move. Move! Amber, is it your turn to serve?"

"Excuse me. Serve?" the floral-spandexed one

responded, indignantly. "As if! Call a catering service."

"It's either you or Janet. One of you better get to the back court and serve!" Diemer roared.

"Hello, wake up and smell the subpoena," Amber snapped. "No pun intended, your jockness, but it'll take a court order to enforce that request."

"Somebody just hit it to them," De instructed, and as Janet whacked the ball netward, we resumed our conversation.

"So what we need is a serious yet untapped issue," I summarized.

"Something to do with fashion," Amber suggested.

"Like a needy fashion-victims' fund," Tai enthused.

"For who, people who shop below Sunset?" De was being sarcastic.

"Or in the Valley," Amber added thoughtfully. "I mean, having access to the best of everything doesn't automatically mean you dress well."

"Out of the mouths of would-be babes," Alana muttered.

"Amber's right," Summer concurred. "Remember that heinous beaded schmata Winona Ryder wore to the Academy Awards?"

"Stop. Wait," I said, holding up my hand. Out of the corner of my azure eyes I saw the off-white orb sailing my way. "Oh, no!" I exclaimed as it bounced off my upturned palm and continued its relentless journey. "Fashion already has a charity," I pointed out. "They do that thing in New York every year where designers donate all these major threads and you can buy them at a fraction of their cost. No, we have to come up with something new. Something that's like unique, yet urgent and fun."

"Fat chance," Summer grumbled. "I mean, unless some gross new disease is discovered by this afternoon. And how excellent are chances for that?"

"All the good causes are already taken," Alana agreed.

"Face it, Cher," Amber attempted to summarize. "Your little dream of hosting a happening gala is just that. A dream. Just another teen fantasy, like winning a weekend in Waikiki with Keanu or hangin' backstage with Beck or having those Barneys from Publishers Clearing House schlepp a billboard-size check up your driveway."

"O ye of low frustration tolerance," I counseled my crew. "It is always too soon to give up."

While I did not share their negativity, I so understood it. Idling in the steamy sunshine, soaking up smog-enhanced UV rays while constantly trying to avoid being hit by a wildly careering ball was getting on my nerves, too. But defeat—unlike determination, depilatory, and defrizz—is so not in my vocabulary.

Yet, for a moment, I was stumped. I knew I had to find a way to raise the sinking spirits of my peers, to jack them up emotionally and get them back to the crucial planning phase of the choice charity blowout I was now committed to organizing. But how? I turned to De.

"I totally echo Cher's sentiments," my best bud asserted as Coach Diemer's whistle sounded again.

"Oh, what does she want now?" Baez grumbled.

"Ask me if I care," Summer snapped.

"Okay, gold team. You win!" the coach shouted.

"We win what?" Amber wanted to know.

"I think she means the game," said Janet. And when everyone looked at her, all, Duh, excuse me, what are you talking about? she added, "You know, the *volleyball* game."

"We're winners?" Tai was bewildered.

"I knew that," Amber insisted.

De and I exchanged glances. We were way in sync now, totally attuned to each other's positive vibes. If we were going to throw a truly crushing bash, we had to seize the moment.

"Hel*lo*," I cried out to my teammates.

"People," De called.

"As Coach Diemer so eloquently announced —" I said.

"As if we need to be reminded," my telepathic t.b. interjected.

"We are winners," I continued.

"And we won without even trying," De pointed out.

"Or even knowing," I added. "So, when it comes to creating a truly excellent charity event, imagine what we can do if we just set our heads and hearts to it!"

"We're winners." Tai broke into applause.

"Totally," Janet concurred.

41

Then Summer, Alana, Baez, Tiffany F., and Shawana joined in. And finally, even Amber started clapping. Only Tiffany Gelfin's hands were still. But that, and the pained expression on her face, was due way more to the loss of two acrylics than any lingering pessimism. There was no doubt about it. One way or another, we'd find a worthy charity. And then we were going to throw a frantically fresh affair.

Chapter 4

*T*he next day, while waiting for social studies to begin, Dionne and I focused on Maura Leslie. While our peers compared designer labels, engaged in pointless games and cosmetic repairs, and held hyperactive cell phone conversations, we began the difficult process of evaluating the needs of our makeover candidate.

Miss Geist's assistant was cluelessly clothed again, in a shapeless embroidered blouse, long ruffle-hemmed skirt, and these orthopedic suede sandals that made Birkenstocks look cutting-edge chic. It was embarrassing even for a would-be teacher. But, oblivious to both her fashion failings and the manic high jinks of the class behind her, Maura was busily scribbling on the blackboard.

"Actually," said De, studying the style-challenged

teaching assistant, "her figure is doable. A decent highlighting rinse and some volumizing gel could salvage her limp locks. But those rags she's flaunting are totally terminal."

"Color-wise, they're so the wrong season," I agreed, ducking the Frisbee Sean had just hurled at Nathan.

"Too muted, too fragile," De agreed.

"Look at this." I selected a handful of color chips from my Color Me Beautiful kit and fanned them before my bud. "Our Maura is a bold, full-on autumn wrongly decked out in the wussy hues of spring."

"That is so profound," De enthused. "Girlfriend, you have majorly pinpointed the problem."

"It's decorative, not structural," I replied, relieved.

"Also on the plus side," De added as the late bell rang and Miss Geist hurriedly entered, "the girl's got noble eyes. We've just got to replace those random glasses she wears with a decent set of contacts."

I was so engrossed in analyzing Maura's Betty potential that I barely noticed the tall, curly-haired guy in the wire-rimmed glasses who'd followed Miss Geist into the room. His arrival was accompanied by appreciative murmurs from the female members of the class and envious grumbles from the altitude-challenged males among us. The stranger's presence jarred Ryder, who fumbled the Frisbee Nathan had flung to him. With a mindless flick of the wrist, the burnt-out boardie sent the dangerously speeding disk straight for Maura Leslie's poorly clad but viciously vulnerable back.

"Yesterday," Miss Geist was saying, "I promised

you a surprise. And here it is. Or rather, here *he* is," she corrected herself, flushing slightly. "Class, I'd like you to meet—"

"Ruark Rosner," I said, looking up to recognize the smiling, craggy-faced babe Josh had introduced me to in Daddy's study.

"Ruark Rosner," Miss Geist echoed as Ruark's big hand shot out and caught the Frisbee a second before it struck Maura's spine.

Maura must have heard the thunk of plastic hitting the lofty hottie's palm. Startled, she turned. Ruark gave her one of his Lincolnesque grins. Instinctively, the teaching assistant removed her smudged glasses and rewarded him with a fuzzy, unfocused smile of her own. It was so adorable.

"Mr. Rosner is a graduate student in architecture," Miss Geist said, "who is here today to talk with us about maintaining and preserving our precious architectural heritage. Now, I know you've all read about the Llewellyn estate," she added optimistically, "and about the powerful commercial interests that are trying to destroy it—"

"And build like this fly new mall, right?" Sean called out.

"And seriously stimulate the economy by bringing multiple new jobs to our community," Amber added, "as well as broadening our spending horizons."

"Excuse me, but what is the furious fuss? I mean, about saving a little five-acre, fifty-seven-room mansion with swimming pool, tennis court, stables, and formal gardens . . . Hel*lo*, why bother?" Alana asked. "L.A. is furiously littered with them."

"Not like the Llewellyn estate." Ruark spoke up. "Does anyone here know who Lawrence Llewellyn was?"

Most of the class started shrugging and shifting and offering such valuable data as, "Some rich old guy, right?"

But some of us had done our homework. "The *Times* article just called him 'the legendary Lawrence Llewellyn,' " I noted. And some, like Ringo and Janet, had gone way beyond the assignment into like library-land.

"Lawrence Llewellyn was a pioneer filmmaker," Ringo recited, standing and glancing at his notes. "His career spanned fifty-five of Hollywood's most vital years. He started out as a stunt rider in early Westerns."

"He died just a couple of years ago," Janet added. "And like his memorial service was the hottest ticket in town. My stepmother, who is an excellent client of Mr. Llewellyn's former secretary's second husband's daughter's masseuse, could not even wangle standing room for the event."

"That is so tragic," Baez consoled. "My dad said Llewellyn was like some major movie star's grandfather. Only he couldn't remember whose."

"Veronica Vidal," said Maura.

"Really?" This last fact was obviously news to Ruark. He was way impressed. "I never heard that," he said, tossing a major smile Maura's way. "But the rest of it is right on target. Llewellyn died two years ago, at the age of one hundred and two—"

46

"Yuck!" Amber exclaimed. "He must have looked like Raisin Man. I don't think they'll even give you a face-lift after you're ninety. I wouldn't."

"Well . . ." Our visitor kind of blinked at the girl of a thousand faces. "I don't know what to say about that."

"Trust her," Summer urged, halting progress on the unicorn she was drawing on Nathan's hand. "Amber's nose has been under the knife more times than a Canter's bologna."

Ruark slipped off his glasses and studied them for a moment. Then polishing them on the hem of his safari jacket, he planted his towering self on the edge of Miss Geist's desk and returned to his topic. As Ringo had said, Larry Llewellyn—that was what Ruark called him—had been one of Hollywood's great moviemakers. He'd started out in St. Louis, Missouri, working in a nickelodeon when he was just a kid."

"The dude worked for Nick? Get out. Like Nick, the channel. Nick at Nite. I watch that all the time," Ryder informed us. "Go, Ren and Stimpy. I love those little kooks."

Ruark put on his glasses and, running a hand through his sandy curls, tried to stifle a smile. But it was no-go. "Well, no," he said, with this choice grin. "A nickelodeon was where early silent movies were shown. 'Nickel' because you paid five cents to see the movies. And 'odeon' from the Latin word *odeum,* which meant a roofed building where musical performances were held."

"Far out," Ryder said.

Ruark moved on to how the adolescent Llewellyn was so stoked on movies that he decided to head west. He was about fourteen when he hit Hollywood and got a job, first as an extra and then as a stunt man in Westerns that were then being made right in the Los Angeles basin, in the parched canyons of Malibu where, the architect said, the Gabrieleño and the Chumash Indians had settled eight hundred years before.

Next thing you knew, Larry Llewellyn was coming up with story suggestions, and then working on scripts, and then making pictures of his own. He wrote, produced, and directed. At one time he owned his own studio, Llewellyn Magna Pictures, which was bought by a bigger movie studio, making him a millionaire. Around that time, Ruark said, he built his estate. Llewellyn did everything in a big way. So he hired one of the best architects in the world, Andre Hargis, to design the place.

I tuned out as Ruark was describing the details of the mansion and found myself gazing at Maura. Slender arms folded across her dorky embroidered blouse, she was leaning against the classroom wall, kind of wedged between the Declaration of Independence and Miss Geist's collection of photos torn from newspapers. This shot of a Laguna Beach mud slide was fluttering near her cheek, competing with her bland and desolate hair for natural disaster status. But the girl's face was radiant. And totally focused on Ruark Rosner.

"The Llewellyn estate was Hargis's last and best building," the lanky lecturer was saying. "A masterpiece of mission style architecture that deserves to be protected and preserved." And then his wire-rims flashed in Maura's direction, and for this eensy instant he hesitated. And smiled. And lost his place. And cleared his throat.

It was this moment of major eye contact. I turned in my seat and like went spanning the globe. I checked out Alana, Baez, Shawana, Tai, and even Amber, but no one seemed to have noticed the furiously flying spark.

By the time I refocused on Ruark, he was all into this rant about how architecture was as historically and aesthetically valuable as any other art form. And that destroying an original and important building was like trashing a great work of art. Imagine, he said, tearing down the *Mona Lisa* because you wanted to build a McDonald's in its place. Or smashing Michelangelo's *David* to make room for a CPK.

A couple of Barneys went, "Yeah, so? You'd be down one statue but up like barbecue chicken and pineapple pizza."

"The Llewellyn estate is not just a physical property," Ruark pressed on, "it's also an historical site. A place where for over fifty years Hollywood's best and brightest gathered. Where generations of film people—moguls and bit players, stars and stunt men—rubbed elbows, exchanged gossip, caught up on industry news, shared stories . . . stories that often became memorable movies. Llewellyn and his wife,

Honey, always invited young people to their home. And these newcomers to the trade were able to listen and learn from the best in their craft. So this house, this architecturally important property, is also a vibrant Hollywood landmark. It deserves a better fate than the one Ronald Blunt has planned for it—to become rubble under a redundant and artless marketplace. The Llewellyn estate should be protected and preserved."

"Totally!" my homeys agreed. Maura broke into spontaneous applause. Ruark sent her a grateful glance, and the teaching assistant turned redder than Amber's roots. Which is so not difficult. "What can we do? How can we help?" everyone was calling out.

"Hello, excuse me!" Amber interrupted. "Do you happen to know which emporiums Mr. Blunt's mall intends to feature?"

Ruark shrugged. "The usual, I guess."

"What, like trendy designer money-pits?" Summer asked.

"With like a frappuccino boutique?" Tai ventured.

"And maybe," Baez added thoughtfully, "some state-of-the-art cellulite disposal salon?"

"That would be so wicked," Alana decided.

You could totally feel it in the room. The sudden mood swing from landmark preservation to frenzied consumerism. One minute it was all stop Ronald Blunt and safeguard the Llewellyn estate and the next it was omigod, a new Prada in the neighb', I've gotta get my credit limit raised. My peers were perilously torn between saving a building and spending a bundle. But De and I were indifferent to the debate.

"Ruark Rosner?" she wondered aloud.

"And Maura Leslie," I finished the thought. "Girl-friend, I think we've stumbled onto a potentially classic couple."

"And," De reminded me, "my total ticket to the Whitney blowout."

Chapter 5

*H*ours later Dionne and I were heading
across the Quad toward student parking. De had
arrived early that morning and snagged a prime spot,
but the lot was full by the time I arrived. So I was
going through my Vuitton epi leather wallet in search
of my valet parking stub.

It had been another rich, full, educational day.
We'd done social studies, algebra, and art appreciation. Lunched on boneless, skinless chicken breasts
perked up with mango-kiwi-mint salsa. And after
setting up our after-school appointments—for me
this meant confirming a four-thirty with Fabianne,
my masseuse—finished up with P.E., science, and
English.

"Generally I respect Mr. Hall and think he's cute for
an aged baldy, but the man needs a brutal reality

check," De was saying. "I can't believe he's still serious about that letter-writing campaign."

"I fully second that emotion," I said, crumpling up a couple of old Saks receipts clogging my purse. "I was sure he'd change his mind by today. It is such a whack assignment, trying to figure out what we have to complain about. Especially when he won't accept getting lukewarm cappuccinos with like watery foam in the cafeteria as a legitimate human rights violation."

The sky was flawlessly blue. You could catch a glimpse of it here and there above the gray layer of late afternoon smog. As usual, the impeccable acre of spewing fountains, floral-bordered lawn, and cedar chip paths we were crossing was being tended by a flock of uniformed gardeners. They looked way subdued in their gray coveralls amidst the blazing tropical bouquet of designer-decked students.

"And when I brought up maintenance personnel uniforms?" De reminded me, tactfully indicating a couple of landscapers taking a beverage break.

"I know," I said, finding my ticket at last. "My heart totally went out to you. I had to restrain myself from protesting."

"Everyone was all, 'But, Mr. Hall, you just don't get it. Beverly Hills is a radically chronic community.' Hello, like who would curtail our freedoms except the occassional grumpy parent? Imagine writing a letter to your senator saying, 'My stepmom grounded me for wearing baggy jeans to my grandparents' recommitment ceremony.'"

"The man is out of touch," I concluded as De and I

paused for two ninth-grade fans who wanted to know where we'd gotten our heart charms and whether we recommended Panténe hair products over Salon Selectives.

"Actually, I found it hard to concentrate on English today," I confided to my t.b. after we'd ended the interview and autographed the souvenir Polaroid the duo had insisted on, "after noting the sparks that flew between a certain tall, dark, and craggy architect and our forthcoming beautification project."

"I know," De agreed. "I was like all immersed in social studies, too. Did you see the way Maura blushed whenever Ruark glanced her way?"

"How def is fate? Here we were, working out the details of Maura's renovation, when in walks a way props partner for the girl," I reflected. "Now all we have to do is spruce her up and put her in Ruark's path."

"Which may present an icky obstacle," De pointed out, "since we're virtually clueless about where the height-enhanced Baldwin may show up next."

"Better hurry, Cher," a too-familiar voice called out. "Only three shopping hours left before dinner."

My jubilant mood took an unscheduled dive. "Josh!" De cried with unsettling zeal. "What are you doing here?"

"I've got to pick someone up," my generically clad former stepsib said.

"I know your social life is meager, Josh," I remarked, taking in his archaic khakis, faded flannel plaid shirt, and scuffed boots, "but wouldn't you have better luck in one of those dark, poetry-reciting venues where it's any badly dressed ship in a storm?"

Daddy's favorite prelaw student chuckled like he thought I was kidding. "I'm here to pick up my friend Ruark Rosner. Have you seen him?" he asked, falling uninvitedly into step with us. "You met him the other night, Cher. He's the grad student I brought over for Dad to meet—"

"That would be *my* dad," I reminded him. "And actually, yes, we saw and heard the boy earlier today, in social studies class."

"I can't believe it!" De exclaimed, overcome by the coincidence. "We were frantically just discussing him."

"Really?" Josh looked surprised, then he got all pleased. "Hey, that's great. His talk must have gone well. So he won you over?"

"Mega-profusely," De offered.

"I hope he can be as persuasive on Friday night," the stepspawn mused.

De and I glanced at each other, then started to grin, then turned back to Josh. "Excuse me, did you say . . . ?" she began.

"That you know where Ruark is going to be this Friday night?" I said.

"And like with whom?" De added sensibly.

"Well, yeah." Josh was touchingly bewildered by our eagerness. "He'll be with me and a group of other concerned citizens. We're trying to organize the effort to preserve the Llewellyn estate. Friday night's our first committee meeting."

"Tscha!" I furiously rifled through my purse. "Where exactly is this conference being held?" I asked, flipping open my creamy leather date book and uncapping my gold Montblanc pen.

"Friday. And today is Tuesday," De muttered, her julietted fingertips rushing through the arithmetic. I knew what she was thinking: That we had a scant three days to redo Maura and get the renovated teaching assistant to Josh's meeting, where Ruark could witness the miracle of our makeover. "That doesn't leave a lot of time," she concluded.

"Well, no," Josh agreed. "Blunt is determined to level the place as fast as possible. But if we get the landmarks commission involved, they can hold up his demolition permit, at least until an historian researches the property." He looked from me to De and back again. "Wow, I'd never have guessed you guys would be interested in a project like this. That's what Friday's meeting is for. Bringing people together to stop Ronald Blunt from desecrating this beautiful estate—"

"We're fiercely in favor of beautification and bringing people together," I interrupted his rant. "So where's the rendezvous?"

"Yeah, right," my weird former brother said. But he gave us the address, and as I jotted it down, I got this viciously killer idea. Struggling with Mr. Hall's assignment would rob De and me of precious moments, time better spent bettering Maura. All we needed to snag a decent grade was something to complain about. Who better to help us be discontent than the prince of protest, himself?

"Josh, De and I so want to come to your rally or whatever," I assured him, "only Mr. Hall gave us this terminally lame homework. I mean, he wants us to find a flaw in our privileged environment and write these impassioned letters to officials, spurring them to corrective action."

"But this being the greater Beverly Hills area, there is fully nothing to complain about," De supported my plea.

"How about the destruction of the Llewellyn property?" Josh ventured, sort of sarcastically. "It's something that's happening right here in your community, an issue that hits close to home. You could write letters to city officials demanding that they thwart Blunt's efforts to turn the estate into a shopping center."

"It's so simple. I'm like totally plotzing," De said.

"That's it." I smacked my forehead, but lightly. There was no need to stimulate the flow of natural oils and get all shiny-browed about it, but I was fully psyched.

Dionne in her little red Mercedes and I in my chronic white Jeep were in cellular contact all the way home. Except for like five minutes, when I was pulled over by this motorcycle cop, who tried to hand me a citation for not wearing my seat belt.

It was so bogus. Of course, I was wearing a seat belt. It was this mango one that perfectly matched my fun Christian Lacroix top. Which was why the officer hadn't noticed it. So first I had to explain how I'd had this assortment of seat belts made up to match my most choice ensembles. And then I had to pop open the glove compartment and show him the colorful array. And finally he tore up the ticket.

It wasn't his fault. What does the LAPD know about accessorizing?

By the time we pulled into our respective circular driveways, De and I had firmed up our agenda. Now that we had a proper issue to protest, we wanted to get Mr. Hall's assignment out of the way. After that we would finalize plans for Maura's makeover and then find a way to get her to Ruark's Friday night meeting.

Homework shared is homework lessened. So, while I rescheduled with Fabianne, De convinced some of our assignment-burdened buds to join us at my Karma Drive casa for a fervent letter-writing fest. An hour later five of us were crashed out in my pastel pink room with enough chilled diet Snapple and warm cheese nachos to get us through the first draft.

"Okay, should we extoll the virtues of Lawrence Llewellyn or trash Ronald Blunt?" I asked, fingers poised above the keyboard of my power PC.

"Who are we going to mail these letters to?" Tai wanted to know. Nacho crumbs dotted her bluish lip gloss, and a slender strand of bright orange cheese trailed down her chin.

"Josh suggested we focus on the press and city hall personnel," De responded. "I think we should brutally blast Blunt."

"And recklessly burn our bridges?" Amber called from my Laura Ashley-skirted dressing table, where she was sampling my cosmetics. "I mean, what if he decides to open a mall on some site nobody cares about and then bars us from shopping there?"

"So you're saying what, Amber?" De asked. "That we should suck up to Ronald Blunt so that if he builds a future Galleria over some abandoned toxic waste dump, our plastic will be good there?"

"Maybe we should leave Blunt out of it," Baez mused, reaching forward to pull the cheese string off Tai's face. "We could just focus on the importance of preserving that architect guy Hargis's masterpiece."

"I can't believe you ate that!" Amber shrieked at our peroxided pixie-cut-coiffed bud. "That was second-hand cheddar, Baez. You are so gross."

"Gross?" Baez tossed her platinum head, setting multiple metal earrings jangling. "And what do you call that red eye shadow you just smeared all over your lids?"

I glanced at Amber and saw which of my makeups she was testing. "It's not eye shadow. It's creme blush," I said. "Hello, people. I need some positive input here."

"Well, Wei Jingsheng sent his complaints right to the guy who put him in prison," Janet, the raven-haired brainer, reminded us, "so maybe we should send our messages directly to Blunt."

"Yes, but that's because the Wei man wasn't allowed to go to a wider audience," De pointed out. Sitting cross-legged on my bed, my chenille velvet Ralph Lauren throw tossed casually over her French terry canvas-trimmed drawstring leggings, she was browsing through my CD collection. "I bet if he could've he would have wanted the press to publish his remarks. Remember what Mr. Hall said. We live in a free society where people are not sent to prison for airing their grievances. So we can use the media. And we can tell our politicians what we want."

"And that would be what?" I coaxed, trying to get my group on track again.

"To stop an egomaniacal, greed-based mall-builder from demolishing one of our community's architecturally excellent and historically significant buildings," Janet summarized.

"And?" I prompted.

"To get through this dumb assignment with a decent grade," Tai offered.

"Tscha!" I said. "And since each of us has to submit a letter, we can focus on different aspects of the issue, okay? And maybe, Janet, you could kind of go over our first efforts and like proofread for accuracy, spelling, and grammar?"

"Totally," the Asian American princess agreed, brushing a nacho speck off the stretchy black lace sleeve of her slinky Kenzo top. "Plus, if nobody else wants it, I'll tackle mall congestion in our area," she proposed.

"And I'll trash Blunt," De volunteered.

"Ooo, I wanted to do that." Baez was disappointed. "Maybe I'll just rant against those who place the interests of commerce above aesthetic considerations."

"Whatever," said Amber. "I am not taking a stand against one of the country's most powerful real estate developers. I could, however, do a short piece on how unfair it is that his seventeen-year-old daughter got this major modeling contract when her nose is like two inches below Beverly Hills beauty standards."

"I think Kiki Blunt's long, narrow honker is wickedly distinctive," Baez objected.

"You also think jewelry should be worn by the pound," Amber shot back. "Four pairs of earrings, one nostril stud, an eyebrow ring—your face alone could set off an airport terrorist alert."

"Yuck, that reminds me," Tai announced. We all turned toward her. "Nothing." She squirmed under our stares. "Just I've got to get a new outfit for my aunt Natalie's independence celebration. She signed her divorce papers yesterday, and her support group is throwing her this bender at Spago. But I hate shopping—"

Everyone like gasped.

"Well, not *hate* exactly," Tai quickly amended. "I'm just so bad at it. I mean, I like cruising the aisles and getting schpritzed with fragrances in the cosmetic department and riding the escalators and the credit card part. I just get overwhelmed when it comes to choosing clothes."

I was moved by the girl's raw honesty. And something more. Tai's dismal confession reminded me that another reluctant shopper required my aid: Maura Leslie. I found myself wondering whether I could assist two birds with one stone. Whether Tai's needs and Maura's could be harnessed to serve a single chronic plan. And then I went, like, duh, of course!

My peers had been staring at Tai with compassion and pity, when suddenly she switched gears. "Speaking of benders, though. For our assignment, I'd like to tell about how that guy Llewellyn was so helpful to young people who wanted to break into the movies, inviting them over to his house and all, and how this place that's going to be torn down was the scene of all these intense Hollywood blasts back in the old days," she announced.

"Not even!" De exclaimed, momentarily bruising Tai's feelings. But it was not our choice-challenged bud she was addressing. Brandishing this old CD, De went, "I can't believe it. Cher, you've got *The Bodyguard* soundtrack."

"You gave it to me for my eleventh birthday, De," I reminded her. "You've been a furiously loyal Whitneyite since back when we wore preteens."

"Frantically," she acknowledged, then lowered her voice to a desperate whisper. "Which is why we've got to get started on Project Maura. Winning that bet with Murray is a total must. I love the flawed boy, but no way am I going to skip a one-night-only Whitney Houston flickfest to watch two massively obese losers assaulting each other."

"Don't even think about it," I advised softly. "I already had this choice brainstorm that involves Tai. Anyway, we're just about ready to shred this assignment and move on. Okay," I addressed my troops, "we'll compose our letters now. Then Janet can look them over and add any pithy editorial comments of her own. After which we'll come up with a list of local opinion-makers, newspapers, 'zines, and politicians to whom we can E-mail our persuasive statements.

Plus, as Janet suggested, we'll send copies of our complaints to Ronald Blunt himself. Agreed?"

"Agreed!" everyone cried.

"Girlfriends, start your laptops," I said. "The faster we finish this assignment, the sooner De and I can concoct a classic scheme to lure Ms. Leslie to a righteous renovation."

It was nearly dinnertime when Amber and Baez left. Janet studied my fervent plea to preserve the Llewellyn estate. "Polite, yet pithy," she observed. Then she suggested some minor changes. I gave her revisions the green light, and she bailed, carrying printouts of our forceful correspondence. Only De, Tai, and I remained. It was time to plot the beautification of Ruark Rosner's soon-to-be irresistible new squeeze.

Chapter 6

Maura was garbed in her usual frump-wear on Wednesday when we filed into social studies. Compared to her, Miss Geist's food-stained silk shirt-waist and gum-soled sandals looked bitterly def. As De, Tai, and I moved up the aisle, my heart leaped with the knowledge that today was the last bad-hair day of the rest of her life.

"Did you see the article on Mongo?" Murray asked De as we passed his desk.

"Not if it wasn't in *Vogue, People, YM,* or *W,*" she informed him over the gently padded shoulder of her toast leather Prada jacket.

"It wasn't in *W,*" Sean informed her, flashing this grotesque pulp rag at us, the cover of which was decorated with a trio of snarling, bare-chested mutants in spandex tights. "It was *WWF—World Wrestling Foundation News.*"

"Oh, excuse me. I guess my subscription ran out," De countered.

"No problem." Murray pointed his dimpled chin in Maura's direction and sadly shook his head. "When this folly of yours to convert Ms. Leslie from loser to loqued-out babe runs its course," he confidently declared, "you'll be meetin' Mongo in the flesh."

"And he means *flesh!*" Nathan assured us.

"Spare me while I spew," I said, taking De's arm. She was trembling. "Trust me, girlfriend. You won't run into that repulsive wall of meat unless he shows up at the cineplex. And they'll have to squeeze him into a shirt before they let him in."

"Promise me," De said, gripping my hand.

"It's a done deal," I assured her.

While Miss Geist lectured us on good citizenship, I flipped through the week's department store sales brochures, reappraising the items De, Tai, and I had selected for Maura last night. Macy's at the Beverly Center had some stylish threads at twenty percent off, as did some of the better boutiques in the Beverly Connection across La Cienega. There was no time to send for corrective clothing from the handful of mail-order catalogs I'd brought to class, still I browsed them for inspiration. I also perused the latest issues of *Hairdo* and *Coif,* seeking a style that would make the most of Maura's forlorn follicles. Before I knew it, the bell had rung. "Good luck," I whispered to Tai, gathering up my books and brochures.

"Don't fail us," De urged her.

Our social studies teacher and her assistant were chatting at the front of the room. "Er, excuse me, Miss Geist," De interrupted them. "Can I talk with you a moment about . . ." She glanced at the Declaration of Independence. "About the pursuit of happiness," she said. "Outside. Privately. For just a second."

Miss Geist seemed surprised yet flattered. "Of course, Dionne," she said, her hands fluttering at her collar. "Maura, will you excuse me for a moment? I'll be right back."

"Sure, no problem," the teaching assistant said.

I lingered in the doorway as Dionne ushered Miss Geist into the hall. On cue, Tai, who was still at her desk, began to softly weep.

Maura Leslie turned immediately toward the distraught girl. Tai's head was in her hands, blue-streaked hair falling dejectedly over her desolate face. The yellow-striped shoulders of her Tommy Girl jersey shook slightly as she cried.

"Tai?" Maura murmured compassionately. "What's wrong?"

"I need someone to go shopping with me this afternoon, and all my homies are like brutally booked," my bud revealed in a voice quavering with misery. "I feel so alone. So abandoned. Worse even than my aunt, who just got divorced and is having this frantic bash at Spago Friday night. And I want to really, really look good, or at least better than the pizza they serve there, which is way choice."

Maura began wringing her unmoisturized hands.

As her oversize glasses slid down her somewhat oily yet petite nose, her classic eyes seemed to mirror Tai's misery. She'd need a matte-finish base, I thought, to soften that sheen.

"This afternoon is the only time I've got to find a drop-dead ensemble for the extravaganza," Tai continued, snuffling loudly. Streaks of cobalt mascara were washing down her distressed face. "But I'm like a major cadet when it comes to decision-making. And there's no one to go with me!"

"Oh, please don't cry, Tai. I mean, it isn't worth it. It's just a dress," Maura pleaded.

I gasped, uncontrollably. "Hello, excuse me, Ms. Leslie," I announced from the doorway. "It isn't just a dress. It's like shoes and a bag and earrings and possibly a cashmere cardigan—"

The look of relief on the teaching assistant's face told me I'd made a monster blunder. "Cher. Why, you're one of the best-dressed girls in the class. You can help Tai, can't you? She's your friend, your homely."

"Homey," Tai corrected her.

"And she needs help. The kind of help I . . ." To her credit, the girl indicated her nasty attire with a hopeless sweep of her arm. "I can't really offer," she said. "Can't you go shopping with her, Cher?"

"No!" Tai and I shouted at once.

"I mean, I've got to study for this test," I improvised.

"She's got a piano lesson," Tai blurted out simultaneously.

"A piano test," I explained.

"And anyway, if you're so concerned, Ms. Leslie," Tai whined in exasperation, "you could have at least *offered* to go with me."

"Well, I would if—" Maura began.

"I accept!" Tai shouted, jumping up and hugging the startled assistant.

"Excellent!" I exclaimed. "I'm sure you two will have a fun time shopping together. Okay, well, see you later. I mean, good luck. And thanks, Maura, er, Ms. Leslie. You won't regret this charitable act. I totally promise you."

"It was such a narrow escape," I told De several hours later. The two of us were sipping mocha frapps in the Attitudes section of Macy's. We were sitting on these little gold chairs between a wall of Dana Buchman separates and a rack of Anne Klein II, waiting for Tai to deliver Maura into our hands. "I should never have interrupted them. I just got so freaked because Maura was like not reacting to Tai's distress the way we planned."

"So you told her you had a piano test?" De asked, awed. "And she believed you? That is so inspired. I would never have thought of that." She glanced at her watch, the same TAG Heuer Formula 1 Chronograph with orange dial that famed makeup artist Kevyn Aucoin wore in this *Vanity Fair* ad. "They should be here in two minutes," she said.

We turned simultaneously toward the escalator. Like a mushroom cloud over a nuclear bomb testing site, an explosion of unnaturally red hair rose slowly into view.

"Could it be?" De began.

"Amber," I affirmed. Although this enormous pair of Fendi Occhiali shades hid half her face, she was squeezed into the same tiger-striped, fringe-hemmed tube dress and leopard lace-up boots she'd worn to school.

"What a surprise," she said, stepping off the escalator and peering over her dark glasses at us. "I hardly expected to bump into a pair of hardened mall-bashers like you at a prime shopping venue like the Beverly Center. I ran into Janet at CPK. She sent those E-mails to Ronald Blunt," she informed us. "I'm glad I signed mine, A Friend."

"Janet forwarded our complaint letters?" I asked as De's bony elbow nudged my pink-lace-Anna-Sui-swathed rib cage. Beyond the tacky tentacles of Amber's red locks, I saw Tai and Maura Leslie coming up the escalator.

"Whoops, gotta go," said De, grabbing my frappuccino venticup and handing it, along with her own, to the tawdry intruder. "Don't forget, Ambular, you take the Ventura Freeway to get to Griffith Park. Just in case you want to return that ensemble to the zoo. I mean, it's so close to feeding time."

Just then Tai called out to us in this loud, faux innocent way, "Why, Cher, De, what are you doing here? Look, Ms. Leslie, it's Cher and De."

"Speaking of the zoo," Amber remarked, studying the duo.

"Did I say size nine?" I asked my homey with a satisfied smile.

"Girlfriend, you were so correct," my bud confided,

measuring Maura with her eyes. "That loose, flowing frock briefly deceived me. I thought she was a ten."

"A ten? Excuse me?" Georgette of the Jungle broke in. "You can't be talking about the teaching assistant from planet Clueless."

"We weren't scoring her Olympic excellence," De responded. "We were estimating ensemble size."

"Get over it," Amber said. "You really still believe you can convert that walking slipcover into a stylish Uma?"

"Ignore her, De," I advised, "like common sense and good taste have. Amber," I addressed our negative nemesis. "We've got a job to do here. It's a grueling task that calls for ingenuity, commitment, and probably a decent volumizer. Now, either sign on or ship out."

"Hey, you guys." Tai was carrying a shopping bag. She shook it at us. "Maura helped me pick out something for my aunt's party. It's so totally geeky, it's like next generation."

The teaching assistant laughed, giving me a rare op to study her teeth. They were food free, pearly, and properly racked. The burgundy-hued lipstick I'd chosen for her would accent them to the max. And entirely go with the simple dove gray suit I'd selected from the sale rack.

"I really don't know that much about clothes," Maura confessed.

"Duh," Amber mumbled. I shot her a meaningful look, and she rolled her eyes but put a sock in it.

Maura was saying, "How did that piano test work out?"

With quick precaution, De stepped in front of Amber. "Cher furiously aced it. So we rushed right over here to help you. I mean, to help you help Tai."

"Well, whew." Adorably, Maura pretended to mop her brow. "No kidding, that's great. Boy, we could use some help. Right, Tai? But how did you know we'd be at Macy's?"

"Cher's way psychic," Tai blurted.

"That and, um, actually, I had to pick up this amazing suit," I said. "But, silly me, I paid for it and they took out the shoulder pads at my request and like hemmed it and everything, and then I noticed it was a size nine, and I so wish I knew someone with brownish hair and pale green eyes who'd look wicked in dove gray, because it's a seriously slammin' outfit but destined to languish in my closet unless I gain a gazillion pounds."

"Or find someone who might want it," De suggested. "Er, you wouldn't be a size nine, would you, Maura?" she asked, all wide-eyed.

"Omigod, she is!" Tai shrieked.

"I think I'm going to hurl," Amber grumbled. For a moment I thought I'd have to take action, but then the big-haired one peeked out from behind De with this completely counterfeit smile and went, "Gosh, Ms. Leslie, this must be your lucky day."

"Well, er . . ." The teaching assistant scanned our eager, hopeful faces. "I could use something new, I guess."

So we marched her into the dressing room, where De produced the slinky, burgundy silk DKNY blouse her mom had donated to the cause. And I revealed the choice, strappy heels I'd snagged at the Charles Jourdan table.

While Tai and Amber zipped and buttoned the grinning girl into her new dove gray garments, De and I began unloading my backpack. Having placed her glasses on one of the tufted dressing room chairs, Maura watched in nearsighted wonder as we set out a selection of costume jewelry, name-brand scarves, my blow dryer, headbands, and sundry hair aides, plus a Vuitton makeup bag bursting with the earth-tone cosmetics my color charts had decreed.

"They're called accessories," I explained, tilting my head to study Moira's bare but beaming face.

She laughed again and self-consciously ducked her head. "This skirt feels like silk," she murmured, smoothing the lush fabric over her narrow hips.

"Duh, that's because it is," De said. "Satin-lined silk linen."

"Oh, but it's kind of short, isn't it?" Maura protested, but her eyes were aglow as she studied her sassy new look in the dressing room mirror.

"Lucky you've got great legs," Tai chirped sincerely. Which sent the pale-skinned teaching assistant into a furious blush.

"Maura, I hope you don't mind my asking," I began tactfully, "but that is your natural hair color, right?"

"If it's not, she's got an excellent case against her colorist. I'd seriously sue," Amber remarked.

Maura ran her fingers through her meager, lackluster locks. "I'm afraid so. Can I tell you something? I've always hated my hair."

72

"I am so shocked." Amber grabbed her heart.

"Well," De volunteered, "we could kind of fool with your follicles, go the Clairol route, but there's this furiously fabu salon not one mile from here, where Cher and I know the most excellent stylist—"

"He owes me a humongous solid," I said. "Well, actually, he owes Daddy, big-time. This client whose rug he burned started bad-mouthing him all over town—"

"Your hairdresser set fire to someone's carpet?" Maura was all dazed and confused.

"No," De gently interpreted. "He permed this person's wig, and she didn't tell him it was a cheap vinyl hairpiece, so it got all fried and the woman went postal on him and demanded this major apology in cash—"

"And Daddy worked the whole thing out so now Petruccio is all, 'Anything you want Cher. Anything you or your friends need,' and whatever—"

"Tell her the part where you have an appointment with him this afternoon," Tai prompted.

"Oh, yes, don't skip that part," Amber said sarcastically, rolling her bovine brown eyes.

"Well," I began, "I do have a date with the king of color at . . ." For authenticity, I glanced at the gold Rolex Daddy gave me for winning Miss Congeniality at my sixth-grade spelling bee. "Hello, what a coincidence. It's in fifteen minutes. And I know that Pet would die for a chance to transform your lame mane into a majorly trippin' coif—"

"Does anyone have like a Rolaid? I'm totally going to cack," Amber remarked.

As De elbowed the loose-lipped, leopard-booted loser, Tai started going, "Oh, please, Ms. Leslie. When it comes to follicle repair, this guy is the furious flavor of the month, especially for thin, snaggled locks. He's like Rogaine Man. And you so need a buff new hairstyle to go with that seriously dope ensemble."

You could see Maura melting like a mood candle in a spa sauna. "You really think so?" she asked, and she was ours. On the way to Petruccio's, De and I did our accessories show-and-tell for her. We draped scarves, hung jewelry, suggested headgear, coordinated cardigans, and generally demonstrated how to turn a simple hot suit into several stellar outfits.

"How adorable is she?" I marveled two hours later, as Pet applied a finishing schpritz to Maura's highlighted and restructured mop. "I'm viciously kvelling," I said, clutching my homey's hand.

"She may be our best yet," De affirmed, giving my digits an emotional squeeze. "I am way choked. But our do-good work is so not over. We've still got to get Maura and Ruark locked in for a bona fide date."

"Girlfriend, it's in the Prada bag," I predicted.

Chapter 7

*W*e spent Thursday morning brutally basking in acclaim. At school everyone was all, "Did you see Ms. Leslie?" and we were all, "Hello, see Ms. Leslie? We *did* Ms. Leslie."

And then we got all this, "Get out! For real?" and kids would break out their appointment books and electronic organizers and laptops and go, "Oh, please, please, please, can I schedule a makeover with you?"

Except for the wobbly way she walked in her new stiletto-heeled sandals, Maura's renovation was a clean success. Still, De and I couldn't resist making additional suggestions and corrections throughout the school day. Like by ten A.M., her raisin-hued, hydrating, stay-put lipstick had been nervously nibbled to a memory. So, at least twice before lunch, we had to signal the girl to reapply. Then there was the smudge of creamy camouflage base on the neck of her dusty pink cardigan, the heinously flopped lock of highlighted hair falling over her enhanced eyebrow, a chipped acrylic crying out for glue . . . What bogus brainer said you can't improve on perfection? As if! Looking def is way high-maintenance.

Between second and third periods, De and I were flanking Maura as she moved through the boisterous school hallway. I wanted her to get used to navigating in high heels and without those hugely random specs of hers. So De gripped the renovated TA's glasses while I guided her through the milling peer groups and nerd clusters cluttering our school corridor.

My bud and I were used to the whistles and encouraging comments that greeted our passage, but Maura was adorably flustered by the attention she was drawing.

"It takes a little getting used to," De comforted the blushing girl, "but after a while you'll hardly notice it."

"You also have options," I instructed. "You can be all aloof and above it, like you're so busy and basically on another, higher level totally, or you can kind of smile and like every once in a while remember to nod and maybe offer a gracious little wave or whatever. Some of the comments are really random, though. So don't hesitate to, like if someone gets too familiar, just go bitterly icy and frost them."

"Yo, yo, De," Murray's adolescently cracked voice

rang out behind us. "Wait up, woman. You shorties heading for Mr. Hall's class?"

"Here, like watch this," De said as she turned to confront her squeeze. In predictably drooping jeans and an awning-striped XL Karl Kani shirt, the ear flaps of his colorful knitted Andes mountain cap flapping, Murray headed toward us. Similarly attired except for accessories and headgear, Sean, Nathan, and Jesse were with him.

Dionne cocked her head, placed her hands on her hips, and sent the boy a look. Murray's mouth fell open. His eyes creased with pain.

"Brrrrrr," the long-haired Nathan shivered, and fell back, crashing into Sean and Jesse.

"I could never do that." Maura was way impressed.

"Word up, who's the loqued-out new mama?" Sean called, tightening the front knot on his Tupac headrag.

"Frost him," De urged our attitude apprentice. But close to laughter, Maura shook her head, then turned, smiling, toward the baffled boys.

"It's Ms. Leslie!" Jesse said, so flustered he nearly dropped his portable CD player, catching it seconds before it clattered to the floor.

"Naw, naw, naw, that ain't her." Sean refused to believe it.

"It's the haps, bro," Nathan confirmed.

Tears sprang to Murray's eyes as he recognized the teaching assistant. "Whitney Houston? I'm going to have to sit through like twenty hours of sister bonding and chicks dissing men? No way—"

"That's just *Waiting to Exhale*," Sean tried to

77

console his partner. "But then you got Denzel in that preacher movie. He's phat—"

"Plus the *Bodyguard* soundtrack was like an MTV steady, with major chart action and radical radio coverage," Jesse added. "I can get you the CD."

We left Murray and his brat pack in the corridor. He was viciously hyperventilating. Then, just as Maura hobbled into the teachers' lounge, clutching the can of root-penetrating provitamin formula styling mousse I'd handed her, De's boy-toy had a flashback.

"Wait. Hold up. It ain't over," he called out, fiercely grinning. "You still got to get her romantically hooked up."

"Yeah"—Sean brightened, too—"by Saturday!" The Y chromosome crew slapped palms, knocked knuckles, and started cackling all around, then disappeared into Ms. Hanratty's algebra class.

De looked at me, all ashy and alarmed. For an ugly moment it was like she'd been whomped by the panic ball Murray had tossed her way, and all the spunk and confidence was whooshing out of her. "Cher, that's the day after tomorrow," she whispered.

"Exactly," I reminded her. "And in a little while, like after Mr. Hall's class, a light lunch, science lab, and maybe a game of volleyball or some other recreational activity, we'll return to my hacienda to plot tomorrow's triumph."

"Of course." My girlfriend's natural blush returned. "We've got over forty-eight hours. What was I thinking? Maura and Ruark are a lock."

The day flew like hot Pepsi from a shaken can. Before the start of Mr. Hall's class, Janet handed back the homework she'd so excellently edited so that we could sign our letters and turn them in. Mr. Hall, looking like a Gap billboard in his frayed corduroy jacket and khakis that could actually have *been* James Dean's, was way impressed with our efforts. He thought my buds and I had come up with a fully unique and frantically important issue.

In the five minutes it took the shabbily attired English instructor to look over our assignments, the classroom turned into this beehive of activity. Tai broke out her box of colored felt tips and started drawing this excellent rendition of Spawn on Ryder's arm. Amber filled her plastic retainer with bleaching gel and slipped it over her teeth. De was trying gold alphabet decals on her acrylics and looking bummed because she couldn't fit all the letters of *Dionne* on one hand, unless she squeezed two *n*'s on a single nail. Thinking that I'd work on my self-improvement to-do list, I took out my journal and pink feathered pen. After an idle moment—I mean, how much bettering did I really need?—I asked Janet why she had E-mailed our notes to Ronald Blunt.

"It was a total accident," Janet confessed, studying the selection of hair accessories on her desk. Picking a pale blue scrunchie from the bunch, she slipped it over her slender wrist and began to comb her long, silken hair. "I mean, I was editing them on my computer, on E-mail, figuring we'd send them after class and I hit send now instead of send later." She shrugged. "I don't think it's that big a deal. Except, they also got sent to this list of city hall officials I was gathering." The brainer began to braid her hair. "But, hey, we're not Wei Jingsheng or Nelson Mandela. Who's going to care about what a bunch of high school kids have to say?"

"Janet, that is so defeatist." I was shocked. "We count. We're viciously relevant. It's just like I said in my letter. I mean, how much do we spend in shopping centers across this nation on a regular basis? Hello, like plenty. And let's say if Ronald Blunt, who owns a gazillion malls, goes against our wishes and destroys the Llewellyn estate, we could like threaten to stop shopping, big time."

"You just said that for the letter, right?" Janet asked cautiously, fastening her long, lustrous braid with the baby blue scrunchie. "I mean, stop shopping? Cher, you wouldn't."

"Of course not," I told her. "I said, 'threaten to.' But don't think that wouldn't count."

Janet stood up and twirled. "You like it?" she asked as the single raven-hued braid whipped the air.

I quickly scrawled in my journal: "Remember, you count!" Then, feather pen poised thoughtfully against my cheek, I went, "Extreme honesty?"

"Not if it hurts," Janet said.

"Not even. The braid works, but scrunchies are so, I don't know. Like all fabric-covered rubberband-y. I'd have gone for the lavender velvet ribbon. It's way more supportive."

After school De and I drove over to my house. "It's not going to be all that difficult," I assured her as we swung through the oversize double front doors. "First of all, Maura is in this fiercely upbeat mode. Her makeover has frantically boosted her confidence. She's like a former bus rider suddenly cruising the freeway to success at the wheel of a Porsche Boxster with the top down and 'I'm Every Woman' blaring from the CD player."

"Totally," De enthused as the clicking of our sandal heels echoed through my white-marble-floored entrance hall. "Plus we've already discovered that she's not only open to suggestions, but is a grateful and rapid learner—"

"Okay, so, two." I ticked off the positive aspects on my manicured fingertips. "There is this way obvious attraction. You saw how Maura was eyeballing Miss Geist's guest lecturer."

"Like Amber eyeing a lamb chop," De agreed as we both bent to unbuckle our shoes. "But I didn't notice whether the bespectacled boy returned the sparks."

"Well, he didn't rebuff them," I pointed out, kicking off my Manolos and stepping down into our enormous sunken living room. I wriggled my toes in the ankle-deep carpeting and then went, "And three-ish, because of her clear and present interest in the hottie, as well as her basically do-good nature, it won't take much convincing to get Maura to go with us to the Llewellyn rally."

"So, it's what we do to get Ruark to notice *her,*" De decided, joining me.

"Excuse me," I said, "but did you notice anyone *not* noticing her today?"

"Good point," my bud agreed, sandals in hand. "So probably he'll notice her. Maybe even recognize her."

"Like she'll look vaguely familiar." I plopped down onto the wraparound sofa. "A bit like that blushing young teaching assistant he met at Bronson Alcott High, and yet . . . way more classic somehow."

"Totally." De sat on the floor, facing me with her back against the huge white ottoman. "So, let's move on to locking in their actual date. That's the crucial part. He's got to ask her out."

"They'll need an occasion," I proposed.

"Like what, a socially relevant play? A serious movie? A major concert?"

"Some mega-irresistible special event," I mused. "Something that taps into whatever they have in common."

"I just had this tragic thought," De announced, flinging herself flat on her back into the plush ecru carpeting. "What if Maura already has a date? I mean, it's Friday night, after all."

"Not a chance," I assured my supine t.b., clutching an antique silk pillow trimmed in gold braid against my washboard-flat abs. "Maura Leslie is one of your total Whoopee, it's Friday. Time to kick off my clogs and crash types. She's probably planning to like pick up a pie and zone on tabloid TV."

"You think?" my homey asked, propping her bare feet, with their recently painted blue toes, onto the edge of the sofa.

"Trust me," I said.

A thunderous clap of noise interrupted our scheming. De and I shrieked and scrambled to our feet.

It was Daddy. "What!" he hollered. "What's wrong with you? What are you screaming about?" His pale, chunky face appeared at the arched entrance to the humongous room.

"What's wrong with us? Duh, he*llo*," I said, clutching my heart. "You only like slammed that door so hard, this entire casa went into quake mode."

De waggled her fingers at my father. "Hi, Mr. Horowitz. Phew! I totally thought we were sliding into the San Andreas Fault. Did you have like a rough day?"

"You want to know what a rough day I had?" Daddy demanded.

De nodded compassionately, as he flung his Bugatti briefcase onto one of the brocade-upholstered chairs flanking the marble mantel of our faux fireplace.

"Of course we do, Daddy," I said, flopping back onto the couch to give him full attention.

"Don't ask," he fumed. "You don't want to know."

"Hello, repressed stress can send your pressure soaring, Daddy. Spill your grief before you trigger a cardiac event," I urged him.

"Aw, what's the point?" Daddy griped. "You work, you slave, you plea-bargain. For what? So that a gang of spoiled brats can send poison-pen letters to your client and sabotage your career? What's this world coming to when a bunch of high school kids, who should be spending the best and most irresponsible

83

years of their lives on fun, start trying to change the system?"

Daddy was really upset. "Can I get you like a diet iced tea or something?" I asked.

"I don't want tea. I want a milk shake," Daddy grumbled, "with real ice cream, not frozen yogurt, and real milk, not skimmed, and real chocolate syrup, not sugar-free! Aw, look. I'm sorry for ranting at you."

"I know, Daddy," I said, patting the sofa beside me.

"What a day." Loosening his yellow silk Saint Laurent tie, he sheepishly shuffled over to the couch and sat down. "So, enough about me. What are you kids up to?"

"Helping a teacher," De said, "a recently renovated Betty."

"She's this buff education major who's been assisting Miss Geist." I added, "Plus, De and I and some of our t.b.'s are thinking about throwing a charity bash, as soon as we decide on a righteous cause."

"That's my little do-gooder," Daddy said, ruffling my highlighted hair affectionately. Which I like so hate. It totally makes me feel like Daisy, the Wonder Pony. "Anything I can help with," he promised, smiling at last, "just let me know."

First period Friday morning, while Mr. Hall was taking attendance, I phoned Josh. I needed one final piece of information before De and I formally invited Maura to the meeting.

"Hello, what?" the faux bro answered in this raspy murmur, after like three rings.

"Josh, what's wrong with your voice? Why are you whispering?" I asked.

"Cher. I should have known." His hushed tone switched from cautious to complaining. "Nothing's wrong with my voice. I just don't want to speak louder than my lit professor, who just happens to be in the middle of a terrifically interesting and probably important lecture."

"Whoops, you're at school. My bad," I murmured. "Okay then, don't talk. Just listen, okay? Here's why I called. De, Tai, and I are coming to your affair tonight and we're bringing this golden guest, who's like all that about preservation. So I just have to know, is your friend Ruark Rosner involved or anything? Just grunt—one for yes, two for no."

"Involved in what? The meeting, yes," Josh hissed.

"Duh, hello, I knew that," I reminded him. "I meant, like is he crushed on anyone? Does the boy have a main boo, a major big, a serious squeeze?"

"No!" Josh growled. "That's what you called me for?"

"As if!" I protested. "I just need to know what Ruark's hobbies are. Like what activity or event would he furiously enjoy?"

The boy got all bent. "I can't believe you called in the middle of class to ask such an asinine question!" he raged.

Mr. Hall got to my name just then. "Oh, get a life!" I hollered, then clicked off. "Er, not you, Mr. Hall," I said, with a full-out smile for the flustered teacher.

* * *

We couldn't blow off P.E. or duck science lab without chancing a grade-lowering disaster. So it wasn't until lunchtime that De, Tai, and I tracked Maura to Miss Geist's classroom, where she was grading papers and munching a soggy tuna fish sandwich.

"That little white T-shirt looks trippin' with your new suit," I called from the door, "but Ragin' Raisin is so the wrong lip color. Way too stark. Let me see if I've got a warmer shade in my bag."

Maura glanced up, momentarily startled. Then she threw us this welcoming smile and removed her random specs. "I went back and forth between this"—she proudly plucked the simple shirt—"or my patchwork denim blouse with the red and pink rickrack piping."

"Not even," De gasped involuntarily. "I mean, you were totally on the money to go with the tee," she hastened to assure the girl.

"We were just wondering whether you've got any plans for tonight," I said, fishing my makeup kit out of my backpack.

"That you couldn't instantly unload if like a chronic alternative surfaced," Tai added.

De handed Maura a clean tissue. "Wipe," she suggested as I pulled out my matte finish lip rouge and retractable lipstick brush.

"Well, it's Friday," Maura said, obediently removing the dark lip stain, along with this wayward speck of tuna and mayo. "Usually, I like to just stay at home and relax."

"Hello!" I said to De.

86

"And like curl up with the remote and maybe send out for a pizza?" my bud probed.

"My favorite Friday night thing to do," Maura confessed, then added by way of explanation, "I don't actually know too many people out here yet."

"Well, you know us, and we need you a lot more than *ET* or *Extra* need the rating points," De blurted.

"I don't think I understand," Maura said.

So, while I applied a fresh coat of Revlon's super lustrous Iced Mocha to her lips, and Tai brushed the teacher-to-be's hair to a glossy radiance, and De soft-penciled her eyebrows in this dope Ranch Mink shade, we gave her the four-one-one on the meeting. And of course, as I had predicted, Maura's resistance to the plan was less than zero. Especially after we got to the part where Ruark was going to be there and had practically organized the event.

"And he was asking for you!" Tai ad-libbed, over-eager to close the deal.

Maura's mouth fell open under my lipstick brush. "Really?" she asked, smudged but delighted.

Realizing her error, Tai glanced desperately at De and me.

"Psych!" De went to Maura. "Not actually, Ms. Leslie, but we are way confident that given a decent op he would have, right, Cher?"

With fully touching trust, the educator's excellently made-up eyes fastened on my own cornflower blues.

"The boy definitely sent sparks your way during his lecture," I confirmed, "and that was *before* your hair, makeup, and ensemble selections underwent drastic corrective measures." Gently, I dabbed away the Iced Mocha smear with a clean tissue and repenciled Maura's lips. "If I were you, I'd check to make sure what you wear tonight is flame-retardant, if not fully fireproof," I said, stepping back and studying the transformed teaching assistant with like abundant satisfaction. "The way you look now, girl-friend, those sparks could viciously ignite."

Chapter 8

*I*t was Friday night in Westwood. Which meant that the usual crew of UCLA students—faded flannel shirts tied around their waists, hiding the undesirable labels of their generic jeans—were joined by trendy restaurant goers, movie-buffs, and boutique-hopping tourists. The village sidewalks were clogged with more randoms than a Lollapalooza in the Valley.

Young, attractive, and vibrantly decked out in colorful designer casuals, my buds and I owned the jammed streets. Crowds parted as we—with the exception of Maura, who looked fierce in her dove gray duds but was still a little wobbly on her Jourdans—swung confidently toward our appointment with destiny.

Westwood is like the pedestrian capital of Los

Angeles. Everyone walks. You say, "Valet parking?" They say, "Duh." So we had to leave my Jeep and Amber's tangerine Miata at a *meter*—which was like miles from our destination and, of course, took only cash. If Maura hadn't come up with the correct change, we'd have practically had to panhandle for coins.

Anyway, after a fifteen-minute excursion in footwear designed for beauty, not hiking, we stopped before this Starbucks wannabe called Café Olay. I checked the piece of paper on which the address of the meeting was scribbled. "A caffeine dispensary? What a surprise," I said sarcastically. "Where else would my ex-stepsib spend a Friday evening? I just hope it's not open mike night."

De pressed her flawless forehead against the dark bean bar glass. "Typical Westwood milieu," she declared. "Major espresso machine, movie posters on a dimly lit brick wall, little round stainless steel tables—"

Taking her tape recorder from her purse, Amber joined De at the window. "We're at Café Olay in Westwood," she said into the little machine. "It's this goth scene, all dark and trendy—"

"Amber, you're not going to do that all night, are you?" De said.

"Excuse me, your Dionne-ness," the piqued poetess grumbled. "I must have missed the election where you were voted head of the Let's Not Embarrass Ourselves in Westwood squad. I just want to make one more note. Note," she said. "No wonder everyone around here gets all flipped over the rain forest. They've got more ferns in there than in the entire Amazon Basin."

It was surprising that any plant life survived. The retro cafe we entered was viciously murky. Most of the light in the place came from tabletop candles and this one bluish spotlight, which was focused on a dark-haired hunk in T-shirt, jeans, and Hush Puppies. The square-jawed hottie, who bore a fierce resemblance to Andy Garcia, was clutching a microphone and sitting, sort of, semiperched on a tall stool. "So what we need, as I see it, is to raise money and consciousness," he was saying in this wickedly husky voice amplified through whistling speakers.

The meeting had apparently started without us.

"Not necessarily in that order," the trippin' babe added. A ripple of laughter and agreement ran through the audience. A ripple of "He*llo,* who is *that?*" ran through me.

Tearing my eyes from the Baldwin, I picked my way through the gloom. Everyone was in basic coffee-house threads: dark, subdued colors, primarily black. Black tights, black ankle boots, black high-heeled loafers, black tees, black microminis, even black khakis. It was all dark and trendy, like a funeral by Calvin Klein.

I felt a tug at the back of my hot pink crop top. "Cher! Over here." Janet and Baez had arrived before us and snagged a couple of prime tables.

"What have we missed?" I asked as we joined our t.b.'s.

"Well, your step gave this impassioned little speech about forming committees to protect the Llewellyn property," Janet filled me in. "He's like head of the legal fund. And then there was a hip-hop duo who did an antimall rap which, I personally felt, was way disrespectful to committed shoppers in the audience like Baez and myself. And then the tall, curly-haired guy we saw in social studies class delivered this passionate pitch—"

"We missed Ruark's speech?" I asked.

Baez said, "Not really. It was a total Xerox of Tuesday's rant: Hollywood history, architecture as art, mall-bashing. You know, educational, inspiring. Whatever."

"I'll be right back," Maura whispered, teetering at the table's edge. "I think I've got a blister on my ankle. I'm just going to find a Band-aid."

"So now," Janet continued as the teaching assistant limped loungeward, "this Andy Garcia junior clone, who wants more kids to get involved in the project, is like talking about ways to attract them."

"Attracting people is so not the boy's problem," I mused aloud, turning in my seat to focus on the spotlit babe.

"Cher?" This shadowy stooge suddenly blocked my view. "I can't believe you actually showed up."

"Josh?" I said, trying to peer around his lanky, denim-clad form. "Try."

"Well, I'm impressed," he conceded.

"Be still, my heart," I grumbled. "Excuse me, Josh, but I totally told you we'd be here. We are frantically committed to this project."

"Hiii-iii, Josh," my easily stirred buds sang out. Ever since grade school, my intimates have thought the faux bro was monster cool. "As a matter of fact," De, his biggest fan, said, "we've already barraged city hall and Ronald Blunt himself with pages of protest, right, Janet?"

"I E-mailed a batch of majorly moving letters yesterday," the Hongster confirmed.

"That was you?" Josh was seriously stunned. "I can't believe it. You actually took my suggestion? I heard about the letters, but I didn't think you guys had written them. I mean, Cher, I can't believe you went out on a limb that way. I can't believe that you didn't crumble under the pressure—"

"Excuse me. Is your believer broken or what? My crew and I are way action-oriented," I informed him. "We live in the solution, not the problem. We're deeply committed and seriously serious. Now, who's the bona fide Brad up there?"

Josh glanced at the hottie in the spotlight. "That's Jeremy. He goes to Grearly Academy."

"He's got like the best voice," I said, referring to the deep, laryngitis-like sound rasping through the speakers. "Grearly? But that's like an all-male prep school," I gasped. "You mean that fully hunked-out babe is a *high school boy?*"

Just then Ruark reappeared, and the deceptively doable muffin handed the microphone to Maura's soon-to-be big.

"Thanks, Jeremy. And everyone," the towering grad student began. "Okay, we're here to save the Llewellyn estate. I've talked about its architectural relevance. Josh has filled you in on the legal measures we're taking to get Blunt's demolition permit denied.

And Jeremy and the Grearly crew are working on ways to spread the word among young people in our community. So"—the bush-jacketed babe scanned the audience—"are you ready to join us? Are you willing to pick a committee and get to work? Any questions, ideas, problems?"

A couple of people called out, "Yeah, we're ready. We're with you." A couple more went, "Who cares? I thought this was poetry night." Then this one guy hollered, "I'm already doing whales, owls, and sea turtles. Now I'm supposed to save real estate, too?" And this irate girl went, "Sea turtles? Please. What about the California condor? What about the Spanish lynx, the Malayan tapir?" "Okay, say we salvage the building. What happens to it then?" someone else wanted to know. "Hello, does anybody even care about the ozone layer anymore?" a shrill frizz-head whined. And then it was like everyone had something to say. Even if it was just to tell someone else to shut up and sit down.

Ruark's easy smile opened into this startled O. His granny glasses glinted as he surveyed the mayhem. "Hey, one at a time, okay?" he called. But no one was listening to him.

"Fur reeks!" A pale Betty at the next table pointed accusingly at the hairy collar of Amber's peppermint-striped pants suit.

"Oh, yeah?" Amber stood and shouted suddenly, "Well, Cher wears leather!" Tai and Janet tugged at her stooged-out jacket, pulling her back into her seat.

94

Suddenly, this shrill, piercing whistle lacerated the din. De and I looked at each other. "Maura?" we both mouthed. And sure enough, there was our golden girl, standing just out of spotlight range, over near the espresso machine, kind of startled herself at the stunned silence that followed her blare.

"Excuse me." She cleared her throat. "I mean, I have this suggestion."

Ruark reached out his hand to her, and she stepped forward into the blue light. "Well, someone asked what would happen to the house, if we did save it. So, I was thinking, what about using it as a school, a place where young filmmakers could study and work? Which was kind of what Llewellyn himself used it for, wasn't it?"

There was this murmur of interest that grew into an approving rumble. People started getting excited again. Best of all, Ruark was fully focused on Maura now. "That's a terrific idea," he said. "I'd love to work on it with you."

The look that passed between them was unmistakable. The microphone in Ruark's big paw was practically buzzing from the electricity crackling between them. They were a full-on lock.

De and I leaped from our chairs and slapped digits. "I am so kvelling," I joyously confided to my bud. "The woman is more than a successful makeover, she's majorly morphed."

Suddenly this blinding flash of light startled the crushed couple. "Omigod, they're sending visible sparks," I said, awestruck.

"Not even!" De grinned at me and waved her Polaroid camera, from which a classic photo was emerging. "For Murray," she explained. "My man will demand proof of our success."

"Major snaps," I congratulated her.

"Hello," Amber sang out. "Wake up and smell the cinnamon-flecked latte. A picture of two adults grinning at each other like Jim Carrey and Jeff Daniels is so not evidence of an actual date."

"Hello, bite me," De rejoindered, pulling the finished Polaroid from her camera and brandishing it at Amber. "This fully demonstrates Ms. Leslie's boosnagging ability."

Enthused by Maura's suggestion, the café was all in an uproar again. "How about setting up a foundation that could offer scholarships to young filmmakers?" a movie geek in a Steven Spielberg baseball cap asked.

"The Llewellyn Foundation." The studly Jeremy tested the concept aloud. "Outstanding idea," he decided. "But it would take a lot more loot than we've got in the legal fund to set it up."

I don't know if it was the word *fund,* as in *fundraiser,* that sparked my brainstorm or the adorably lost look in the dark-haired hottie's pale blue eyes. "Our charity bender!" I alerted my homeys. "How perfect is it? This is the flawlessly righteous cause we've been searching for!" I cleared my throat and smoothed down my suede Miu Miu mini. "Hello!" I called, standing on tiptoes now and wildly waving my hand.

Jeremy caught my signal. Those azure eyes beamed my way, followed by this unabashed grin. "My name is Cher Horowitz," I announced.

"Cher?" Ruark's overly perplexed voice interrupted. "What are you doing here?"

"Hello, just because we're young, popular, attractive, and outfitted in fun colors doesn't mean we're all duh when it comes to boring stuff like community affairs," I informed him. "In fact, I and my associates hereby volunteer to put together a fund-raiser that will furiously shred the city. A frantic fiesta to raise consciousness and cash for the Llewellyn Foundation!"

Maura was the first to applaud. Then like everyone was going, "Yess! Beautiful. A charity fund-raiser! Organized and run by concerned young people. Monster idea!"

"The trendy Westwood boite was majorly moved by our bash proposal," Amber hollered into her tape recorder.

For once the girl was money. Everyone was tilted over the plan, except for my ex-relative. "Cher, are you sure?" Josh questioned me again.

I rolled my eyes and sighed impatiently. "Excuse me," I said. "Of course, I'm sure. De and I and all our buds are way experienced in this area. We've been to countless charity affairs. Plus, who knows more than we do about getting someone to write you a really big check?"

"Or sign a credit card receipt or make a cash contribution," De added.

"And speaking of supportive parents," I continued, "Daddy already said he'd help. So we are brutally at go."

"I can't believe Mel's going to back you on this one," Josh insisted.

I scanned the randomly clad boy, my annoyance eased by pity. "I know the word *fun* totally panics you politically correct types, Josh," I said. "But just like find something real to wear and get ready to party down at the mega-blast of the season."

During my conference with Josh, Ruark's voice was droning at the mike. Excellent as I am at multitasking, I caught little of what the tall one was saying. "Amazing" was one word I heard. "Star" was another. And then, all of a sudden, Ruark bellowed, "Veronica Vidal," and De grabbed my arm and, shrieking excitedly, viciously squeezed it.

I turned toward the spotlight. There was Daddy's favorite movie star, her famous red hair trailing down her back, which was stylishly bare, except for two little sequined spaghetti straps that so said Mizrahi. The reason that pale back was turned to us was the reason De had pinched my biceps. Veronica Vidal was administering this huge hug to our own Maura Leslie.

The entire place was frenzied. "What happened?" I asked my homeys. The question set off a fierce duh-fest with shrugs all around. Finally the scarlet-clad celebrity answered it herself. With raised arms, she faced the rowdy crowd. "Look at her," I whispered to De. "She's like Daddy's generation, and there's not an ounce of flesh trailing from her triceps. We've got to get her trainer's name."

"I came tonight both to thank you and to apologize. To thank you for your efforts on behalf of my grandfather's estate. And to apologize for not knowing about those efforts until earlier this evening, when Maura phoned me." Veronica clasped Maura's arm affectionately and, hanging onto the blushing girl, told everyone that she'd be happy to join the fight to save the old house where she and Maura's mother, who it turned out was Veronica's childhood friend, had spent some of the most fun days of their youth.

After this really brief but heartfelt pep talk, another hug for Maura, and a jiggleless wave to us all, she left the bean bar with this little mob of well-dressed friends. The Café Olay crowd was totally stoked and buzzing.

"We have only one more thing to do here tonight," I confided, pulling De to her bronze DKNY-sandaled feet. "Much as it pains me to even utter the phrase, Amber was right. That Polaroid won't convince your wrestling-obsessed honey. We need to document an actual date request."

"But how?" De wanted to know as I whisked her through the throng toward the espresso bar, where, I'd noticed, Ruark had ushered Maura the moment Veronica was out the door.

"With this," I responded, waving Amber's mini tape recorder. I'd snagged it a minute ago, while Amber was arguing with the fur-fuhrer at the next table about whether or not Veronica had appeared in a What Becomes a Legend Most? ad.

Even in this dimly lit goth pit, I'd seen the way Ruark was eyeing Maura during Veronica's speech. I'd noticed him taking a little electronic organizer out of his pocket. I'd seen his face lit by the digital datebook's green glow as he checked his schedule. Every matchmaking bone in my furiously toned body told me that the tree-tall boy was ready to pop the question to our transformed teaching assistant.

This was the moment. I was sure of it. I clicked on the tape machine.

"So, then you're free tomorrow night?" Ruark said as my best bud and I sidled up to the espresso bar.

Maura was so cute but way naive. She shrugged, blew her hair off her face, and went, "What's tomorrow, Saturday? Um, Saturday night? Definitely. I mean, yes, I'm free. I mean, if it's a Saturday night, you can definitely count on me being free."

"Works for me." Ruark laughed. "So, is seven o'clock okay?"

Maura nodded.

No, I thought, don't nod. Say yes. Say it aloud. Say, Yes, Ruark, I silently urged.

"Seven's great, Ruark," the girl said.

I squeezed De's hand in this burst of gratitude. She shrieked. Maura and Ruark turned to us.

"Got it!" I exalted. "Thanks, you guys."

"Tscha!" De said, and we slapped a limp but heartfelt high-five.

I took the mini-cassette out of Amber's recorder

and gave it to De on the way to our table. When we got back, the area was surrounded by a horde of congratulatory Grearly hotties. We made our way through the preppy pack and slid back into our seats.

The Grearly guys were all, "Whew, a charity bender. Outstanding idea. A cash bash. Bronson Alcott Bettys, we are with you."

"My pops is head of A and R for Downbeat Discs," one dreadlocked Marley-boy informed De. "I'll work with you on sounds."

"I ran Grearly's Moonlight in Malibu fund-raiser," a wonk in a bow tie was telling Amber as I set her tape recorder back down on the table.

Then, there was Jeremy, pushing through the posse, coming toward me. "Whatever you need," he said, blue eyes locked on mine.

"Then you'll help us?" I asked. It was just a formality. The look on his classic face told me that the boy was already mentally canceling everything from therapy to hockey practice to make himself available.

"Count on it, Cher," he said, in his def sore-throaty way. "I'm all yours."

Returning home in triumph, I discovered Daddy pacing the hallway. He was still in his Armani power suit, although the jacket looked heinously rumpled and his tie had been hurled to the floor, I noticed. In one hand he was holding the deadly remnants of an overstuffed pastrami on rye. In the other was a sheaf of papers, which he started shaking at me like the minute I walked in. "Do you know what this is? Do you have any idea?" he growled.

"I pick hand number two," I grumbled back at him, "the lethal animal-fat sandwich that is sending your blood pressure soaring as we speak."

"Get in here," he ordered, polishing off the pastrami in one vicious bite and stalking into his den. "Sit down." He motioned sternly at the big mahogany armchair opposite his desk. I arranged myself on the handsomely upholstered seat and tried to hold on to the smile that had been on my face when I'd entered our sumptuous hacienda.

"Do you know what I've been doing for the past three hours?" Daddy demanded.

"Well, if you were at your athletic club trying to rid yourself of toxins in the steam room or getting a soothing massage or practicing relaxation techniques with your trainer, you should definitely demand your money back. Because you are so not serene—"

"I was with Ronald Blunt!" Daddy interrupted me.

"Yuck," I said involuntarily.

"My client," he loudly continued. "The biggest, most important, and, at the moment, angriest client I have."

"Ronald Blunt is your client?" I echoed, shocked. My mind began to race. Suddenly, one baffling event after another began to make sense to me. Josh's more-annoying-than-usual behavior at tonight's meeting, for instance. No wonder PC-boy had such a hard time believing I'd be involved in the Llewellyn project. Ruark's similar surprise fell into place. They must have known that Daddy was working for the real-estate developer. Was that what they were arguing about in this very room the afternoon that Josh brought Ruark to our casa? That was the day I retrieved from Daddy's choice Palazzetti waste basket the article about Blunt in the L.A. *Times*.

I gasped abruptly as the final piece of the puzzle suddenly fit. The letters Daddy had gone postal over yesterday. The "poison pen letters" that, in Daddy's words, a bunch of spoiled brats had sent to a client of his in an attempt to sabotage his career. . . .

I was overcome with confusion. Which I so hate. I pride myself on clarity of mind and ensemble selection. But now I was seriously conflicted. I would never knowingly do anything to hurt Daddy. Yet I was fully committed to throwing this do-good bender.

"Do I get a second shot at what's in hand number one?" I cautiously asked. "Like could it be a cluster of very persuasive letters imploring our city officials to stop your most important client from demolishing this aged building and turning five acres of prime Beverly Hills real estate into a shiny new shopping mall?"

"Bingo!" Daddy shouted.

"Whoops," I said. "But, Daddy, did you even read our letters?"

He slumped back into his giant leather desk chair. "Of course I read them," he said, pushing his reading glasses up into his gray hair and pinching the bridge of his nose in this moving gesture of exhaustion. "Blunt told me about them yesterday, but I didn't get to read them myself until tonight."

I got up. "Lean forward," I directed him, stepping around his desk and behind his chair. "I so understand your trauma, Daddy," I said softly, starting to massage his tense shoulders. And while I worked on stress reduction, I explained to him how Mr. Hall had innocently assigned us this difficult homework task. And how hard it was to come up with a decent topic, given the world of luxury and freedom that Daddy and the parents and stepparents of my friends and their attorneys, agents, and brokers had made possible for us. And how all they'd ever asked in return was that we be happy, well-groomed, and get choice grades. "Right?" I queried. "I mean, don't you want only the best grades for your favorite daughter?"

Beneath my strong, julietted fingertips, I could feel the anxiety beginning to drain from Daddy's bulky back. He nodded in response to my question.

"And don't you think these letters, however detrimental they may be to your career and your client's ambitions, are brutally trippin' classics of complaint? And that the points they make are way valid?"

Daddy was practically purring now. "That's just the problem," he said. "I do. If I weren't representing Ron in this matter, I'd be persuaded myself. They're good letters, Cher. In a good cause. But"—his back stiffened again—"I *am* Ronald Blunt's attorney. And I owe him the best representation that money can buy."

"You do, Daddy," I said gently. "But I don't. Remember that charity bash I told you my friends and I were thinking of throwing? And you said you'd support us in our endeavor? Well, Daddy, we chose a cause to crusade for tonight. The preservation of the Lawrence Llewellyn estate."

I went back to my chair and sat down. The little statue of Justice, a blindfolded lady holding these perfectly balanced scales, was sitting on Daddy's desk. The bronze figure was a long-ago gift from Mom. I stared at it now as Daddy leaned forward, elbows on his desk, head in his hands. I wondered whose side Justice would be on in this icky standoff. I wondered what my mom, a total do-gooder as well as a great dresser, would have thought was the right thing to do.

Finally, Daddy pushed back his desk chair and took a deep breath. He picked up the little statuette and turned it round and round in his big hands. "I won't forbid you, Cher," he said. "But I am not happy about this."

The taste of victory had sourly curdled, like a bowl of cream into which some cosmic Urkel had poured pickle juice. I was far from defeated but kind of emotionally wiped as I trudged up our plushly carpeted marble staircase to my room. At the landing, I pulled out my cellular and punched in De's digits.

"Girlfriend!" she exclaimed, all upbeat, practically cackling with glee. "I'm waiting for Murray's call-back. I just beeped my man to break the news.

There'll be two empty seats ringside at Wrestlemania tomorrow night, now that Maura and Ruark are the hottest match in town."

"They do make a wicked couple, don't they?" I said, trying to pump enthusiasm into my lusterless voice.

"Second only to you and the blue-eyed Baldwin," De added loyally. "But, excuse me, why do you sound so brutally blah?"

I clued my best bud in on Daddy's plight. And how influential he thought our letters were. And how reading them had seriously swayed him, but that he had to defend his client's interests anyway.

"Your dad is Blunt's attorney?" De was aghast.

"If we could just find a way to convince Blunt to stifle his mall project, Daddy would be off the hook and totally on our side," I reasoned.

There was a click on the line. "I've got to get that. It's Murray," De said. "But remember, girlfriend, you are not alone. Let's sleep on this dilemma. Tomorrow we'll devise some viciously major scheme to fix it. Things always look brighter in the A.M., even on smog-alert days."

My homey was so correct. The next morning, as the fog cleared from my brain like an updraft over Malibu, I found myself musing on last night's happenings. A certain dark-haired, blue-eyed preppie was first in line on my thought parade. But a quick and brilliant second was Veronica Vidal. I punched in De's number on my way to brush my teeth.

"I just had a visit from the fabulous-idea fairy," I

confided, shaking my head and studying my sleep-tousled yet excellently highlighted locks in the mirror. "Veronica Vidal is like the one person who might be able to entice Daddy to our side."

"How Einstein, girlfriend. Your father is terminally mad for the luscious midlifer, isn't he?"

"He is fully Walter Matthau to her Ann-Margret," I agreed, flipping on my Aqua-Pic and hosing my teeth.

"And she is notoriously charitably inclined. But how are we going to get them together?" De wanted to know.

"Maura," I gargled.

"Excellent. That's the who and how," my bud said. "Now what about the where, what, and when?"

As I switched off the water flossing machine, I realized that clarity had returned. My mind was working flawlessly once more, as clean and sparkling as my incisors. "I'll put on this monster dinner party," I decided. "When Daddy finds out Veronica Vidal is on the guest list, he'll jump at having Blunt join us."

"A way props plan," De agreed. "And like you could invite Maura, too, to make Veronica feel more comfortable."

"Classic notion. If Maura comes," I reasoned, "I could ask Ruark to be her dinner partner. Then we'd have Veronica for glitter and Llewellyn family appeal, and Maura on the academic-emotional front, and Ruark could be our facts-and-figures person. But I can't invite Ruark without asking Josh."

"How perfect is that? Your former step can be

majorly annoying when he thinks he's right," De reminded me. "And he'd like tilt the lineup way in our favor. You'd have five pro-Llewellyn feeders at your table versus only two for Blunt."

"Tscha!" I shouted, psyched. "Plus Daddy is actually only half against us since he read our furiously convincing letters." I paused in reaching for my sunscreen-enhanced hydrating foundation with its specially micromilled powder formula that actually diffuses light and gives you gorgeous, glowing skin. "Whoops!" I went. "Gotta go. I hear Daddy stirring. And I was so beat last night, I forgot to set out his clothes for today. He's golfing at Hillcrest. If I don't get in there fast, he'll mix and match his Greg Norman casualwear with like Valentino's Eurotrash chic."

"Yuck." De fully understood. "You go, girl," she encouraged. "Call me later."

Later turned out to be like almost ten grueling hours later. It was nearly dark by the time I got off the phone with the caterers, florist, and house-cleaning crew, and finally remembered to speed-dial my true blue. "It's all arranged. We're on for tomorrow. Sunday at four!" I excitedly told De.

"Cher? Oh, hi," she said softly, sounding vaguely distraught. "I knew you could pull it off."

"And wait'll you hear," I continued, thinking my excellent news would override whatever was dampening her vitality. "Blunt's daughter, Kiki, who was on the cover of *Seventeen* last month, is coming. Here's what happened: Like I phoned Maura the minute I got off the phone with you. She was so stoked over what happened last night. It was totally adorable. And of course Ruark not only asked her out, he drove her home and was all concerned over her foot, which had a blister on it the size of Amber's ego. Which burst. The blister, not Amber's totally undeserved self-confidence. So, anyway, Maura agreed to call Veronica Vidal. And she's on board. Veronica, not Maura. But Maura's coming, too. Only she's like so overbooked—I'm talking about Veronica now—that tomorrow is the only time she had. So, of course, when Daddy got off the golf course, I told him about my plan and once he heard Veronica was in, he was all yes. So he called Blunt. Who was a major *as if* until Daddy dropped the *V* word. At which point the bulldozing developer said that his daughter was like dying to break into movies and that he'd show up if she could join us and meet Veronica. So it is on! How choice is that?"

"Way," my t.b. underresponded again. I could barely hear her voice, and what I did hear sounded more like flu symptoms than enthusiasm. "Er, I'm like really happy for you," she said in this weird, weepy way. I could hear music swelling behind her, and these deep, rumbling voices.

"De, where are you? What's wrong? What's that noise?" I demanded.

"I'm at the cineplex," she sobbed. *"The Bodyguard* is on. Oh, Cher. We're at the ill-fated love scene. Whitney is brutally firing Kevin. I am so choked. Plus I only brought two boxes of tissues. And Murray's already used one of them."

"Your man is crying?"

Suddenly, Murray was on the phone. "Yo, yo, Cher. You can't be interrupting a film retrospective. Wassup with that? This ain't some action epic like *The Crow*. It's a straight-up drama."

"My bad," I said, way relieved. "Tell De to buzz me after the marathon, okay?"

Chapter 9

   Kiki Blunt was about ten feet tall, if you counted her height-enhancing black platforms and the wicked sequined tiara crowning her acres of platinum blond hair. My formerly sensible stepsib, Josh, could not tear his eyes from her.

   From the moment Kiki arrived at our mansionette, in a chauffeur-driven white Mercedes limo, Josh was straining his neck staring up at the linguine-slim modelette. I mean, if Kiki was all nose—and her honker *was* seriously lengthy—Josh was all eyes and ears around her. The boy was grievously glued to her every simple sentence, almost all of which contained the words "My dad."

   Kiki's mom, Daddy had confided to me, lived somewhere in Europe. She hadn't seen her daughter since Kiki was practically an infant. She'd given up all legal rights to the little girl, Blunt's only heir, as part of a bitter divorce settlement. Kiki's mom got about a gazillion dollars. Kiki's dad got Kiki. And he was ferociously proud and protective of her. Apparently Kiki felt the same about him.

"Is my dad here?" she said, sweeping into the entry hall in this little Anna Sui sequined sleeveless with a teeny black sequined feather-edged skirt.

"Not yet," I replied, extending my hand in gracious hostess mode. In contrast to my guest, I was whitely outfitted in a glittery St. Vincent tank top and slinky stretch skirt by Helena Stuart for Only Hearts. My own long, blond hair was adorned with a feathery white pouf of tulle. "You must be Kiki. Like, duh, how would I know that, right?" I continued, although she was totally ignoring my hand. Maybe she was too tall to see it. She was just staring over my head, scanning our living quarters. "Except that your dad's the only other dad besides Daddy who's due here today," I went on cheerfully, taking her two-inch tricep and leading her into the Great Room. "Plus I've seen you on the cover of *Seventeen,* the back-to-school spread in *Elle,* and read your *YM* interview. Anyway, no, your dad's not here yet, but come on in and meet mine and our other guests."

"You work for my dad" was how she greeted Daddy. I sent him a commiserating look. But the diss, if that's what it was intended to be, went over his nobly styled gray head.

That was when Josh first glimpsed the girl. He'd been simultaneously chatting with Daddy and stuffing his mouth with the slammin' hors d'oeuvres I'd ordered from Tinsel Town's hottest catering service.

"And this is . . . well, just Josh," I said, reluctant to get into how I and the generically suited-up boy used to be related.

"My dad said Veronica Vidal was going to be here," Kiki noted.

"She is," Josh assured her, spraying little half-digested crumbs of puff pastry and poached salmon in her direction. "Can I get you something?" He indicated the tray of steamy gourmet nibbles.

"To eat?" Kiki practically gasped. "Hello, I'm a model. My dad's going to get me into movies. I don't think so."

Josh reddened. "Well, er, good luck in your career," he said, blinking up at her.

Maura and Ruark were on the terrace, catching up on the grievous twenty-plus years of life they hadn't spent together. Maura, her hair pumped with volumizer, her face reflecting the flattering pink of the sparkly scarf I'd insisted she borrow, was leaning against the low brick wall overlooking the pool and tennis courts. Ruark, his lengthy self folded to nearly normal size, was sitting on the wall next to her as I walked Kiki through the French doors.

"So like, my dad never mentioned you guys," she remarked, when I introduced her to the classic couple.

"Probably an oversight," Ruark said, laughing. He remained seated. Which was too bad. If he had stood up, he definitely would have had her by inches and could have looked down at her. Which I had the feeling not enough people did.

"Not really," Kiki rejoindered. "My dad tells me everything I should know about people he thinks I should know about."

"I don't think your dad has met Ruark or Maura yet," I intervened. "They are fully memorable," I assured her. "Maura is the reason Veronica agreed to be here today. And Ruark is a student of architecture and way active in the landmarks preservation field."

"Get out," Kiki said to Maura. "You know Veronica Vidal?"

"Are you sure I can't get you something?" Josh, who'd followed us out onto the terrace, asked.

Kiki turned her giraffe neck and looked down at the boy like she was considering grazing off his scalp. She stared at Josh's smooth brow and slicked-back hair silently for a second. Then, as if some inner radar detector had gone off, she brushed past him abruptly and went, "My dad is here. Hey, Dad, hi. Here I am."

As Kiki strode inside, I could practically picture this giant neon sign blinking across her sequined back, going, Fix me! Fix me! Although my trigger finger itched to dial Dionne's digits, I shook my head, holstered the cell phoning urge, and gave myself a silent "Get over it." There were more important things to accomplish today than planning a personality makeover for an anorexic bimbette with a blond IQ and an overblown ego.

"Baby," this booming voice responded to the tiara-ed teen's greeting. With Josh leading the way, we all followed Kiki back into the house. And there, in a stinging cloud of designer aftershave, was the infamous Ronald Blunt.

Arms extended toward his noodley daughter, the flash real estate developer was Armani-ed to the max, crisply turned out in an ensemble so money that there could've been thousand dollar bills tumbling from his breast pocket instead of a casually draped handkerchief. His black silk shirt was collarless and buttoned to the neck. Big, stiff, and commanding, Blunt was every inch the successful business mogul. But his dark, thick hair, which had been tinted, moussed, and sculpted into a blue-black helmet, and the humongous pair of silver-lensed sunglasses he wore gave him this slightly Darth Vader look. You almost expected him to thunder, "May the deal be with you."

Instead, he appraised his daughter's ensemble and laughingly bellowed, "Jody picked that out for you, right?" Then turning to Daddy, Blunt added, "I got the kid a personal shopper. Can't have her looking like every other bimbo on the block. So, how much is that outfit gonna set me back, kiddo? If I was paying by the yard, it'd be a steal." Then he and Kiki exchanged Hollywood air-kisses, and Blunt looked around for other cheeks to buzz and hands to pump.

"Ron, this is my daughter, Cher," Daddy said proudly.

Blunt extended a manicured paw to me. "Ah," he

crooned, checking me out, "so this is my little pen pal. How are your friends, Dionne, Janet, Tai, Baez, and Anonymous? Those were some love notes you kids sent me."

"Hello, the reason why America is ahead in everything is that we have free speech." I was startled to hear myself quoting Wei Jingsheng. Ruark and Maura burst into surprised laughter. Josh and Kiki both gasped. Out of the corner of my eye, I saw Daddy go kind of white. "Someone famous said that," I assured Blunt. "'Even the freedom to say things that are wrong,'" I continued, then quickly added, "care for a salmon puff?"

"And this is Ms. Leslie—" Daddy kind of pushed Maura forward and introduced her to Darth.

"Maura," Maura corrected Daddy, offering her hand to Blunt.

"Maura," Daddy good-humoredly amended, "is Veronica Vidal's goddaughter."

"The legendary Veronica," Blunt boomed, reaching for Maura's recently renovated digits. "So you're sort of unofficially related to that ravishing redhead who received two Academy Award nominations—"

"Three!" a resounding theatrical voice insisted. "What an entrance cue." Everyone turned toward the blinding red presence posed in the arched doorway. There, in a scarlet bustier and trailing taffeta skirt, her crimson hair anchored by glittering ruby-jeweled combs, was Veronica Vidal herself.

Daddy's eyes did like this cartoon *boing!* as the star swept into the room and headed straight for him.

"You must be Mel," she said. "I've heard so much about you."

"Really?" Daddy gulped.

"Not all of it bad," Veronica teased. "But I do hear that you're a formidable foe in the courtroom."

"But a total pussycat at home," I blurted.

Veronica turned to me. Maura said, "Veronica, this is my good friend Cher Horowitz. It was Cher's idea for us all to get together today to talk about your grandfather's estate. And this is Ruark, who introduced you the other night. You two didn't really get a chance to know each other. Ruark Rosner." Maura's voice went all thick and syrupy just pronouncing her honey's name. Veronica noticed it and gave Ruark this serious once-over, then turned back to Maura, all smiling approval. "Ruark and Josh are the guys behind the effort to save Larry's place."

Kiki Blunt gave Josh this evil look, and he winced under her glare. "Nothing personal," he wussed. "I'm just basically against destroying historical and aesthetically important landmarks."

"Oh, but you eat meat, right?" Kiki accused.

"Not veal," Josh asserted.

With a toss of her rustling red skirt, Veronica finally flashed her eyes at Blunt. "And you," the actress said playfully, "are the notorious land baron who is trying to turn my grandfather's home into one big consumer theme park."

"Yes." The developer grinned back at her. "I thought we'd call it Bluntland. Or do you think Ronaldville has a nicer ring?"

"He's kidding. He's a big kidder," Daddy quickly intervened.

"Dad," Kiki whined, "you said it could be Kiki World."

Blunt winked at his spawn. "Well, here's a promise I *can* keep," he said. "Remember, I told you we'd find you the best acting coach in the business? What would you think about studying with a *three*-time Oscar-winner?"

"Three-time *nominee,*" Veronica responded. "I only won twice."

"Oh, Miss Vidal." Kiki did this little sequined curtsy in front of the dazzling redhead. "That would be so phat."

Veronica burst into laughter. "So . . . what?" she asked incredulously.

"Phat," I translated, "Clean, jammin', golden, cool. Basically, she's thrilled."

"See, Cher knows what I meant," Kiki said sullenly.

"I knew, too," Josh said.

"I'd be delighted to give you a few pointers. Introduce you to my own coach. And my nutritionist. But, darling"—Veronica patted the girl's sunken cheek—"I'm afraid your daddy hasn't said the magic words yet."

"Why don't we discuss this at dinner," I broke in. "This buffet I put together is brutally the bomb."

"Oh, yeah? Who catered?" Kiki demanded.

"I'm afraid I can't stay, darling." Veronica turned to me apologetically. "I have to leave. There's an actors' fund benefit at the Century Wilshire tonight, and I promised I'd stop by. I only got the call this afternoon. But I tell you what." She put one of her firm, slender arms through mine, and with the other she snagged Kiki's elbow. "You're painfully thin, darling," she whispered to the willowy model. "You are staying to dinner, aren't you? I want you to positively stuff yourself."

"I'm a vegetarian," Kiki protested.

"I don't doubt it. You look like an asparagus, darling." Veronica turned to Blunt again. "I'm entrusting Maura to speak on my behalf. Any arrangement you can work out with her, I will completely honor. And, Kiki, darling, let me assure you, I'd love to teach you a thing or two."

"Dad," Kiki called out. "You promised."

"I know, baby," Blunt assured her. "Veronica, why don't we just cut a deal now? I'm no ogre. I'm a reasonable man."

"And you can't afford the bad publicity," Veronica reminded him sweetly. "From what Maura has told me, there's quite an effort under way to stop you. In fact, I believe Cher and her friends have spearheaded that effort with a very effective letter-writing campaign. A friend of mine down at City Hall was terribly impressed by the notes he received."

Daddy gave me this proud wink.

"Mel?" Blunt bellowed. "What do you think?"

"I told you yesterday, Ron," Daddy responded. "It's compromise time."

"Did you hear him?" the real-estate mogul hollered. "Compromise. Here's my deal. I'll leave the house alone. The house and a couple of acres surrounding it. But I want my mall. Give me three acres to build on. I'll even put in a movie theater and call it the Llewellyn Multiplex or something."

"Really, Mr. Blunt," Veronica said, all big-eyed and innocent, "I'm terribly late. Please work things out with Maura and her friends. And I'm sure your excellent attorney will give you the best advice possible. Mel—" With this affectionate little squeeze, she released our arms and swept over to Daddy, the lush red gown swishing in her wake. She took his hands. "Thank you so much for inviting me. I've been wanting to meet you for ages. And I'm not a bit disappointed."

"Really?" Daddy said. He was so cute. "I'll see you to the door."

There was this awkward silence as Daddy ushered Veronica out. "Anyone hungry?" I inquired. "Smash Box puts on an awesome feed. They're the troop who do like Jennifer Jason Leigh's blowouts, and they catered David Bowie's tour-wrap bash."

"Not even," Kiki squealed. "They're like masters of tofu. Right, Dad, Smash Box is so the best."

"Tell me about it," I said. "How incredible are they?"

"Profusely," said Kiki as we led my other guests into the dining room.

"Spill," De commanded a couple of hours later, when the housekeeping crew was wrapping up in the kitchen. I had speed-dialed my main big the minute Maura, Ruark, and Blunt left. They were the last of our guests. Josh had followed Kiki out the door fifteen minutes earlier. She was all in crisis, going, "I can't believe I ate chicken."

"Dark meat. With the skin on it," I reminded her. "And you also had a spoonful of curried lamb."

"Don't tell my dad," she begged me. "I've already beeped my trainer, but I think she lives in the Valley or some other cellular blackout zone. I've got to get to my health club. There's a branch open all night in Westwood."

Josh asked if she could give him a lift to his dorm. "Totally," Kiki pledged. "I should so not be alone now."

"So, did we win, lose, or draw?" Dionne asked me.

"Draw is like the perfect word," I confessed. "As in, Ronald Blunt has asked Ruark to draw up revised plans for his mall."

"Get out," De said. "Ruark is going to work for Ronald Blunt?"

"Duh, as if," I responded. And as I wandered our plushly carpeted indoor acres, supervising the clean-up and nibbling the occasional scrumptious leftover, I filled De in.

"Veronica Vidal totally blew Daddy away," I told her, "and so beguiled Blunt's bony daughter that the girl ate her first real meal since carbo-loading cafeteria macaroni in the sixth grade. Plus, bulletin. Hold on to the brim of your Philip Treacy bonnet, girlfriend. Josh, my public-spirited stepgeek, Josh, enviro-nerd protector of endangered *whatever,* has fallen for the real-estate baron's heinously blond daughter."

"No!" De gasped, as I knew she would. "Not even. Josh and Kiki Blunt? That is so whack."

"Totally," I agreed with my t.b. Snagging a stray miniature brownie off the almost-cleared buffet table, I continued my recap. I moved through Veronica's early exit and how she deputized Maura as her stand-in. And how at dinner, Maura, Ruark, and Josh were all into giving Daddy and Blunt the four-one-one on Larry Llewellyn and his Beverly Hills bungalow, when the developer called an abrupt halt to their lecture.

"'Rosner,' he said to Ruark, 'I've done some research on you. You're an architect, right?'" I told De. "And Ruark goes, 'Well, I'm doing graduate work in the subject, yes.' So then Blunt excuses himself from the table, and three minutes later he's back with these huge blueprints. And then it's like, forget the brownies, the strudel, the little lemon soufflés. So much for dessert. Blunt is clearing the dining room table and showing Ruark his plans for the mall. And the next thing you know, at Daddy's brilliant suggestion, Ronald Blunt challenges Maura's man to come up with a new plan—one that preserves the Casa Llewellyn without destroying Kiki World."

"Kiki what?" De asked.

"Kiki World. Long story, girlfriend. It's Blunt's pet name for his mall," I explained. "Anyway, Ruark is going to do it. It's like this major public relations coup that Daddy devised—on the theory of 'If you've got a lemon, make lemonade.' "

"Excuse me," said De. "I've probably still got dried brain from excessive tear-shedding. While ferociously fresh, the Whitney marathon was way draining. Maybe that's why I'm not following your drift."

"You know," I tried again. "It's like, to Blunt, Ruark was this heinous foe, a sour lemon, a brutally bitter pill. So Daddy came up with a way to sugar-coat the boy. And now Ronald Blunt thinks he's all that because by following Daddy's chronic advice, Blunt has snagged the head of the antimall commit-tee to design a shopping complex that'll look frapp yet leave Llewellyn's estate standing. How cool is that?"

"So we like won the battle but lost the war?" De said.

"Excuse me?" I queried.

"If Llewellyn's hacienda is off the endangered list, we no longer have a reason for throwing our junior charity event, right?"

"Hello, what about the film school Maura sug-gested and the scholarship fund for needy movie buffs? A certain Grearly hottie beeped me a little while ago to say he can't wait to work on the worthy bender with us."

"Jeremy? Snaps, girlfriend. You are so right. With the help of that hunk, his preppie pals, and Bronson Alcott's own true-blue crew, the two of us are going to chair a monster blowout!"

"The three of us," I gently corrected my bud. "Blunt's deal has two stipulations. One is that Ruark

will work up a new set of blueprints for the mall. The other is that Kiki Blunt gets to co-chair our fund-raiser."

"No problem," De declared.

"You haven't met her yet," I cautioned.

"A lemon?" De asked.

"Citrus to the max," I reported.

"Well, girlfriend"—my main big laughed—"let's make some lemonade!"

Chapter 10

*T*scha! The date was set. The committees were formed. The Llewellyn Foundation fund-raiser was a majorly happening event. And so were Jeremy and I.

In the weeks since our first encounter at Café Olay, the savvy Grearly senior and I had been in constant contact. We talked by phone every day and for hours each night. Without even knowing it, we'd put each other on our speed-dialing lists. I was three on Jeremy's, and he was five on mine after I shifted Amber to six.

It was so clean to discover how much we had in common. Like we were talking about if we had a music wish-list for the fund-raiser, who'd be on it. And I'm all, "Aerosmith is hugely over," and Jeremy goes, "Yeah, but how rancid is Jewel?" And we were both, "Oasis would be so dope."

Also, Jeremy lived in Bel Air, just a couple of opulent acres away. And he drove a Jeep exactly like mine, except his was black with a white leather interior, and mine was white with black, and where I had this smiley face decal on my bumper, Jeremy had a Stussy "No Fear" sticker.

And best of all, his mom was in the legal profession, too. I discovered this when I was telling him about the little statue of Justice on Daddy's desk and how much I loved it and that my mom had given it to my dad when he won his first major case.

For weeks every time Daddy picked up the phone at home, he'd hear me conferring with Jeremy. So, like a minute after I told Jeremy about the statue, Daddy picked up the extension and went berserko. "Okay, who's on this line? Cher, are you talking to that bozo again? If this guy keeps calling the house every five minutes, I'll haul the kid into court—"

Then, all of a sudden, there was this other voice on the line. "Oh, yeah? On what charges?" it demanded. And Jeremy went, "Mom, come on. Get off the phone."

"Endangering the welfare of a minor," Daddy shouted. "Intentional infliction of emotional distress."

"I'll countersue for harassment," Jeremy's mother growled.

"I hope you have a good lawyer," Daddy fumed.

"I *am* a good lawyer," she said.

"Oh, yeah?" Daddy challenged. "With what firm?"

"She's a judge," Jeremy said.

"Martha J. Fenster, L.A. County Supreme Court," his mom confirmed.

"Martha Fenster?" I thought I heard Daddy gulp. "Er, this is Mel, Mel Horowitz. I have a case pending in your court. Cher, get off the phone," he commanded. "I'd like to speak to Judge Fenster."

"Call you later," Jeremy promised.

"In a pig's eye," his mother said. But then she and Daddy had their chat, and they discovered that they had lots in common, too. So, while he was not thrilled over our friendship, after that, Daddy was all, "Oh, it's you, Jeremy. Give my regards to your mother."

The week before the scheduled bash, my fellow chairpersons and I met with our underlings at Teed Off, the mammoth Bel Air mansion that Ronald Blunt called home but like anyone else would've called a country club.

Like Daddy, the mall-builder was flipped for golf. His thirty-four–room chateau was set on its own rolling eighteen-hole golf course. As De and I drove along the private tree-lined avenue leading to the big house, sprinklers were watering the greens, grounds-keepers were raking the sand traps, and an army of gardeners were clipping the bushes into Blunt's initials, creating a five-mile hedge of leafy *R*s and *B*s.

In this choice Kamali sarong, and a humongously wide-brimmed straw hat, Kiki Blunt was lounging near the Olympic-size swimming pool behind the house. The Blunts' butler donned a helmet and drove us toward her in a white Mercedes golf cart stenciled with the R.B. crest.

"So you and Murray are a lock for the gala, right?" I made small talk with my bud.

"Damian," De said, referring to the rasta-topped hottie from Grearly, "asked me first." Her hazel eyes sparkled mischievously. "But I would never betray my boo. So, yes, Murray is the man. I assume Jeremy has staked his claim on you?"

I sighed. "Actually, De, although we've talked about everything else in the world, you know, what movies we like, what Web sites we visit—I frequent Fashion Planet, he's all Hugo Boss. But the babe hasn't actually asked me to be his date for the party."

"Not even." My gal-pal was shocked. Then she grasped my hand and went, "Be strong, girlfriend. He will."

As we bumped across the rolling sod, we could see that our party-planning crew had already arrived. They were scattered around the grounds. De's entertainment committee—Murray, Sean, Jesse, Nathan, and De's Grearly guy, Damian—were practicing their swings at a driving range just beyond the pool patio. Tai, Amber, Janet, and Baez, the major players on my team, were in the water, splashing up a storm, while conferring with their preppie counterparts. And Kiki's division—Alana, Brittany, the Tiffanys, and a host of Grearly hotties—were sitting under a striped awning near the tennis courts, checking out a rack of dazzling costumes and accessories.

Only Jeremy was missing. As our event coordinator, he was tied up in a meeting with his mom, my dad, Josh, and Ruark. Daddy and Judge Fenster were helping us iron out the legal details of setting up the Llewellyn Foundation and scholarship fund.

Anyway, as De and I stepped out of the golf cart, Kiki unwound from her poolside deck chair. In just two leggy steps, the mall man's only child was halfway across the pool patio, babbling excitedly at us. "My fashion show is going to totally be the best," she vowed, referring to the portion of our party that she was organizing. "Kate's in. And Nadja. Tyson, who does all the major Lauren ads. And Shalom. And then, Wednesday, I had this brainstorm and decided to switch from our L.A. Leisure theme to Movie Fashions of the Llewellyn Era. Isn't that the best?"

"Movie fashions. That is so clean," I said. "You thought that up yourself?"

"Not even. Josh thought it up," Kiki straightened me out. "It like so goes."

"I thought it was *your* brainstorm." De squinted up at the girl.

"Hel*lo.*" Kiki rolled her eyes. "My brainstorm was phoning Josh. I mean, duh. How much can one person do?"

I patted her hand. "Whoever came up with it, it's a brutally stoked notion." Shortly after my def dinner party, I had diagnosed Kiki's malady. Not only did her dad do all her thinking for her, the ego-bloated Blunt had been her sole role model. Although Kiki had his height, wealth, and bony good looks, her father's brash personality so did not work for her. She swaggered like he did, but she lacked real chutzpah.

Also, knowing that her mom had done this *Let's*

Make a Deal divorce, opting for the big bucks behind door number two instead of Kiki, probably hadn't helped. Basically, the girl was all gall and no guts. I seriously suspected that beneath her arrogant, pushy exterior a wuss was struggling to get out.

In our party-planning weeks together, De and I had worked on the Blunt heiress. Supplementing Josh's nonstop efforts to boost her weight, we'd also focused on upping both her self-esteem and humility. We'd had some small success in all areas. The lengthy one was not exactly plump. But the fabric of flesh over her long bones was beginning to look a little more like velvet and less like tracing paper. Sometimes she actually smiled. And sometimes she acted like the teenaged girl she truly was, all moody, manic, and emotional.

"Did Tiffany Fukashima tell you that her father is, like, the comptroller of one of the major movie studios?" I asked the elated girl.

"Oh, and that they'd get this serious tax write-off by lending us all these fabulous, old costumes they never use anymore? Duh, no," Kiki said sarcastically. Then she broke into one of her new little smiles. "Of course, she did. Tiffany's dad got his people to promise us tons of fantastic frocks from their blockbusters of yesteryear. And I leveraged that donation into getting every other studio in town to practically beg us to feature *their* costumes on our runway."

Kiki opened her palms to us, and De and I jumped up to slap her five. "Girlfriend!" we shrieked. Our raucous cry notified our buds that we were here and it was time to get down to business.

When everyone had assembled on the pool patio, I checked my clipboard and opened the session. "As you know, we are mere days away from throwing the rowdiest charity bash ever. So I just want to make sure we're set. Amber, what's the guest list count?"

Looking every inch the flounder in a yellowish swimsuit trimmed with iridescent green and blue scales, the fashion defective responded, "Invitations bearing the poem I wrote for the occasion went out to one hundred of L.A.'s most charitable partygoers. Has everyone heard my new poem?"

A deafening, "About a million times!" rang out around the pool.

"Well, I thought it was golden," the girl did say so herself, "if a little short. I mean, if some goonball klepto hadn't ripped off my cassette, it could have been an epic poem instead of a measly haiku. But then, how many words rhyme with Llewellyn Foundation anyway?"

"Sensation. Inflation. Relation. Impatient. Elation," everyone started chanting.

"Anyway, we got back eighty-three count on its," Amber revealed. "About six as ifs. And my assistant, Wendell, is doing follow-up calls to the rude ten percent who couldn't be bothered to RSVP."

Wendell was the boy in the bow tie who'd waddled up to Amber at Café Olay. His dad had invented the computer software used for tallying Academy Award votes. So the buck-passing diva had delegated her invitation-list dirty work to the Grearly wonk.

"Eleven," Wendell corrected his harsh manager.

"Eighty-three plus six would be eighty-nine, which leaves eleven percent unaccounted for."

"Excuse me, your nerdness," Amber barked at the boy. "What would I know about percentages, right? I've only had my own credit cards since fourth grade."

"Thank you, both," I said, cutting her off and turning to Tai and Baez for the nosh news. They reported that five of the A-list caterers we had targeted were willing to supply free food for our do. Cakeworks on La Brea, who'd created these arty edibles for Elton John and Christian Slater, were going to do a chocolate mousse movie camera for eighty and this vanilla faux film can that would feed an additional twenty-five.

We rolled along like that for awhile. Then Kiki announced the switch in her fashion show theme, and everyone applauded the girl. She didn't mention whose idea it was, but a few minutes later, as Murray and Sean modeled some of the costumes, putting on a swordfight in their swashbuckler suits, Kiki confided to me, "You know, that guy Josh is way smarter than he looks."

"It's those lumberjack threads," I agreed. "You can take the boy out of Seattle, but you can't take Seattle out of the boy."

Kiki was way impressed. "Did you just make that up?" she asked.

Then De took center stage. Well, center patio, anyway. She looked extremely idyllic in her boxy little lime chiffon jacket and pink stretch twill jeans by Miuccia Prada with this floppy-brimmed, pink-and-green chintz hat we'd found at Julian's, where major cool celebs hunt up funky retro wear.

"As chairwoman of the entertainment committee and daughter of a dynamic public relations queen, I and my moms have contacted every hottie on our wish-list. And I want to assure you that we are going to have more names at our bash than there are plaques on Hollywood Boulevard." De paused and Damian, the Grearly babe, filled the brief silence with resounding applause.

Murray rolled his eyes at the boy and shook his head. De's big was still wearing the big plumed hat and scarlet pirate's jacket he'd modeled moments before, but he'd removed the rest of his historical costume. So now this humongous Nautica shirt was sticking out the flared bottom of the jacket, overhanging a pair of cotton plaid, Ralph Lauren American Collection sports pants, one leg of which the boy had hiked up onto his calf. It was my let-Daddy-dress-himself nightmare come true. "As Ms. Dionne's indispensable second-in-command on this project and the sole man in her picture," he called over the dreadlocked preppie's clapping, "I want to point out that, unlike the Walk of Fame names, our celebs will all be alive."

"Yeah," Sean called, "and you won't be able to walk all over them." Then he slapped hands, touched thumbs, and knocked knuckles with Nathan.

"Word, brah," the long-haired Hawaiian transplant responded.

De cleared her throat. "Hello. I just want to say that there'll be a totally glittering lineup of teen favorites, including Dean Cain, Chris Rock, Brad Renfro, Brandy's little brother Ray J, Jennifer Lopez, Jonathan Taylor Thomas—"

"JTT is gonna be there?" Brittany, the secret *Tiger Beat* reader, like almost threw herself in the pool over the news.

"And," De promised, ten names down the road, "we're going to have some huge surprise guests!"

"Straight up!" Murray winked at Sean. "I'm working on something really *big.*"

Finally, De called on Jesse and Damian, our sounds personnel. "My dad got a major maybe from the Wallflowers," Jesse announced to high-pitched shrieks of ecstasy.

"And my pops has a possible yes from Salt-N-Pepa," Damian informed us. The Y-chromosomal crew bellowed, "Foxes. Yesss!"

We were getting a report from my goody-bag girls, Baez, Tai, and Janet, when Kiki, holding onto her satellite-dish-size hat leaped from her tufted lounge and began wildly waving her scrawny arms. "Over here, Josh!" she shouted.

And there was my grinning ex-bro being ferried down the manicured turf toward us in a golf cart. An actual fleet of carts was heading our way, each driven by a helmeted household staffer. I spotted Jeremy in the second one. The smile on his chronic face told me that the foundation contracts were a go and that he was, as usual, brutally stoked to see me.

Holding this little beige shopping bag, Josh climbed out of his vehicle and headed toward Kiki. "Brought you something," he said to our saronged hostess as De and I exchanged amused glances.

"Get out," Kiki responded, studying the parcel. "It's not from Tiffany's, or it'd be in their cute little blue bag, right? And it's not striped like Fred Hayman's signature packages. Ooo, I know, I know," she said excitedly. "It's one of Dad's favorites. How excellent. It's from Barneys New York, right?"

"Close," said my beaming former sib. "It's from Barney Greengrass, the deli at Barneys New York."

Kiki wrinkled her considerable nose. "You brought me a trinket from a deli?"

"I brought you a snack," Josh corrected. "Well, actually, I brought you leftovers. We finished up our meeting at the restaurant and I was thinking of you, so I had them wrap the remains of this amazing sturgeon and lox sandwich—"

Kiki turned on her pedicured heels and stalked away, with Josh in hot pursuit.

De shook her head, setting in motion a rack of lustrous braided extensions. "It's still kind of hard to believe, isn't it?" she said as we watched the dumbest chase scene since that lame Adam Sandler-Damon Wayans movie.

By that time Jeremy had joined us. He, too, was carrying a petite bag. "Let me guess. Smoked fish from Barney Greengrass?" I said, laughing up at him. The dark-haired hunk looked smokin' himself, in crisp khakis and this vibrant sapphire knit shirt by Missoni, which so accessorized his choice blue eyes.

"Actually, it's from Tiffany's," he said.

"Get out," I quoted Kiki, then foraged through the tissue paper until I came upon this adorable blue box. I lifted the lid. And there, on a bed of cotton, was a little gold charm of Justice. It was this perfect mini version of the same gowned and blindfolded beauty holding her scales that my mom had once bought for Daddy.

"So?" my grinning hottie asked.

"Oh, Jeremy," I managed to whisper, "it so busts fresh." Fiercely touched, I held the tiny trophy up, staring through misty eyes at the golden charm.

"I thought you could wear it Saturday night," Jeremy said. "Er, I mean, I know you're the chairperson and all, and that you'll probably have a million things to take care of, but I was hoping you'd be my date for the bash."

"Well . . ." I wanted to shout out my answer immediately. But I forced myself to hesitate. Counting silently, I cocked an index finger against my cheek, furrowed my brow, and looked furiously intense. Then, at ten, I blurted, "Doable."

"Tscha!" I heard De exclaim as, hand in hand, Jeremy and I strolled the flagstone path leading away from the pool and cabanas out past the sun-splashed golf course.

Chapter 11

"Party down!" Ryder Hubbard, decked out in a royal blue tuxedo and Day-Glo-stickered skates, sailed down the massive mission oak banister and leaped onto the priceless red tiles of the entryway. "How cool is this fiesta?" he shouted, swerving to avoid the table where Amber sat in this poufy, pumpkin-colored dress, checking off the names of fashionable stragglers.

"Did you enjoy the poem that came with your invitation? I thought it was fully publishable," she informed the festive latecomers.

The Llewellyn fund-raiser was held, where else, but in the Llewellyn mansion itself. Although it was in need of serious sprucing and repair work, the Hargis-designed house was so worth saving. It was huge and regal and reeked of Hollywood's Jurassically golden past.

The party venue extended way past the tiled entry hall and oak-beamed ballroom—at one end of which was this def trick wall that folded back to reveal a theater-size movie screen. Opposite that wall, Ronald Blunt's construction crew had installed the stage that Ruark designed and our buff fashion show runway. Immense doors opened from party central onto a massive slate terrace that overlooked a monster garden enclosed by flower-draped walls. The Llewellyn place wasn't as big, sparkling, or groomed as Blunt's property, but it had this strange, crumbly atmosphere that made it seem way more chronic.

The once-staid hacienda glinted with the blinding firecracker pops of frantic photographers. *Extra,* MTV, and *ET* posses roamed the premises. Barbie clones stuck mikes into famous faces. Camera crews were ducking and weaving to get their dizzying party pics. Two hours into our bash, Salt-N-Pepa was taking a break. But the ballroom still rocked with excellently deejayed sounds and boisterous conversational groups stalling the frantic dancers.

"So where do you think they'll put the Escada outlet?" I asked. Surrounded by happy campers decked out in party finery, De and I were taking a breather from the hugs, hand slaps, and arduous appreciation of our endless admirers. We'd briefly shed ourselves of Murray and Jeremy, and were standing on the terrace, staring out at all these antique trees and trellised walls and acres of flower beds dotted with statues of maidens carrying water urns, and boys wrestling snakes, and your basic library-type lions. "I mean," I said, "it's hard to think of this place getting malled."

"Abundantly," De agreed, swirling toward me in her strapless satin shift, its butterfly tulle skirt flaring. The petite ice blue dress so accented my bud's hazel eyes, warm, mocha skin, and long, inky black locks. In the twilight glow, she looked like a birthday cake ballerina lit by sixteen candles. "But you saw the model Ruark made," she reminded me. This miniature rendition of the Llewellyn house surrounded by Blunt's mall was sitting on a huge oak table in the tiled entryway. "There's going to be that big cypress grove separating the shopping center from the film school grounds, so maybe it won't look that weird."

"That shade totally heats your skin," I remarked, adjusting the skinny straps of my own sparkly bronze sheath. I'd been set to wear this killer red dress with a beaded bodice and a pair of dyed-to-match Mizrahi pumps. But the day after Jeremy gave me the little charm, I dragged De over to Rodeo and we scoured the Drive for something breathtaking that would do justice to the golden trinket. I'd tried on a parade of partywear before we found the slinky, sequin-studded, bronze mesh gown I was currently modeling. And it was so worth it. Jeremy's extreme grin and Daddy's frazzled frown told me I'd made another perfect ensemble choice.

"You know, Kiki really came through," De mused.

"Profusely," I agreed. "I caught Linda Evangelista coming out of an upstairs dressing room in this amazing hoopskirt that's like Lagerfeld meets *Gone*

With the Wind. The supermod said that she and her *Blue Velvet* squeeze, Kyle, are doing a Rhett and Scarlett stroll down the runway, at Kiki's suggestion. The girl did a jammin' job snagging those costumes."

"And the models," De added. "I wonder if Blunt will notice his daughter's def doings. I mean, as far as I can tell, she hasn't actually leaned on Mall Man much in the past few weeks. Of course, Josh has been way supportive."

"Hello, did you ever see a fallen baby bird that Josh did not wrap in cotton and feed with an eyedropper," I pointed out. "The bro is a compulsive do-gooder, a way committed Elton when it comes to causes. He sees skinny, he hears, 'Feed me.'"

"Hello, there they are," De informed me, pointing toward an ancient arbor below us.

Platinum hair cascading down her bare shoulders, our co-hostess was sharing a garden bench with my stepsib. He was balancing a plate of hors d'oeuvres on his knees and popping one into Kiki's red-rouged mouth like an edible exclamation point at the end of her every sentence. Wrapped in this bandage-tight, glitzy black strapless, Blunt's willowy child resembled a dazzling caterpillar. Josh, on the other hand, in the Abboud blazer Daddy had treated him to, looked like a fish out of water.

"Excuse me, have you ever seen Josh so deflanneled and denimless?" I remarked as De and I checked out the couple. "Kiki is doing wonders for the boy."

"And it's fully vice versa," my bud pointed out. "She must've gained like two whole ounces since

Josh started force-feeding her. Plus her personality has definitely picked up. She even seems, I don't know"—De thought about it—"less blond."

"This project has made more demands on the pampered girl than any endeavor since she learned to walk. Which was about the time her dad started doing her thinking for her," I commented.

"Figuring things out for yourself is way beneficial," my partner concluded as we turned away from the garden gorge. "Kiki's IQ has gone up with her weight. Brains need food, too."

Facing the ballroom again, I peered between the strolling guests for a glimpse of Daddy. Finally, I spotted him in his white Calvin dinner jacket, proudly beaming. Veronica's red chiffon-sheathed arm was wrapped through his as she chatted graciously with a bevy of beguiled guests, including Mr. Hall and Miss Geist, the Zegna-clad Ronald Blunt, and the long-haired Nathan Kahakalau. I thought Nathan was looking not only props in his deconstructed white suit and splashy Hawaiian shirt, but way tall. Then I noticed that the thong-sandaled boy was standing on his skateboard.

"Mel and Veronica are looking cozy, too." De was scoping the same group. "For a movie legend, the woman is way down to earth. She was fully obliging when I asked her for this gigundo favor."

"She's the bomb," I concurred. "Daddy is so in seventh heaven. Veronica has totally been flirting with him. What did you ask her for?"

There was a ruckus at the front door. It had gotten to be a familiar sound. Each time a major celeb had arrived, whether sitcom Baldwin, runway hottie, or MTV notable, our high school homeys had frantically lost it, greeting the guest with rambunctious zeal. But this wave of ecstasy was tidal. The piercing screeches and squeals, the tumultuous rumble of murmurs, reached all the way out to the terrace.

We could see Daddy's little group all turn at once toward the hubbub. With a reassuring pat of her diamond-studded hand, Veronica released his arm. Then people started swarming around her, and De and I couldn't quite see what all the noise was about.

De grabbed my hand. "This may be it," she whispered, clutching her blue-satin-covered heart.

"This may be what?" I demanded.

"That favor I was telling you about," my bud said, her hand visibly trembling with excitement.

Suddenly Murray pushed through the crowd. He was adorably attired in name-brand black: Lauren linen jacket, flowing Calvin trousers, and a simple Emporio Armani cotton T-shirt, with these loqued-out braided black sandals by Cole•Haan. The buff boy was furiously searching for De. The moment he spotted us out on the terrace, he cupped his hands around his mouth, with its meagerly fuzz-decked upper lip, and hollered, "Whitney!"

"Whitney?" I asked, then went, "Ouch!" because De's tightened grasp had brutally crunched my knuckles.

"Whitney Houston!" my best friend shrieked. "Veronica said she'd try to get the gospel goddess to put in an appearance. Oh, Cher." De was gripping both my hands now, and doing this little trampoline bounce. "You were so right. We have totally tattered every charity gala that has gone before us. Not only have we glommed the coolest lineup of talent since Lilith Fair for our fete, but now we've topped it off with the surprise appearance of the soul Betty of the century."

"You go, girl." With a hug, I released my bud into the care of her boo, and the two of them scooched through the crowd to greet the megastar of stage, screen, and tabloid.

While everyone was heading west toward Whitney, my Grearly Garcia was fighting his way east to me. "Whew, everywhere I went, people were saying what a dope bash we put on," he reported, plunging through the mashing masses. "Thanks to you," my coordinator thoughtfully added, surveying me with full-out pride. Then he checked his clipboard and went, "Okay, the fashion show's slated to begin in ten minutes. Kiki's going to narrate it. And then I booked a spot for De's mystery guest, if he shows up."

"She," I corrected my efficient babe. "It's Whitney Houston. She just arrived."

"Outstanding." Jeremy grinned. "So then she'll be our finale. And Veronica's all set to make her show-me-the-money pitch. But everyone thinks you should say a few words before we begin."

"I don't know," I mused, realizing with this icky tremor of angst that I'd been so busy whipping everyone else into shape I'd flagrantly forgotten to put myself in the picture.

Jeremy sensed my distress, which was totally

momentary. Panic is so not my thing. I'm usually as excellently prepared as a Spago egg-white omelette. But my compassionate aide took my face in his hands. Pinning me fiercely with his sincere blue eyes, the babe went, "Trust me, Cher. You've got to do it. Or this evening will be as incomplete as . . ." He paused, his palms warm against my flawless high cheekbones, as he struggled for the right metaphor. Or simile. Or whatever. Finally, with his full lips a breath away from mine, he whispered in his hoarse, Baldwinian way, ". . . as heinously incomplete as my life was before I knew you."

"Not even," I started to say. But Jeremy drew my face to his. Our supple young lips met. He's a senior, I tried to remind myself, as he wrapped his strong, dinner-jacketed arms around me. He's like already applied to five major Ivy institutions, all of them on the East Coast. Yet within the sequined bodice of my bronze mesh gown, my heart was going like the Energizer Bunny. Could this evening be any more perfect, I pondered, lip-locked in my dark-haired honey's arms.

"Cher!" Daddy's roar broke the spell.

Jeremy and I declinched with a gasp. "Veronica wants you," my red-faced parent bellowed. "She's up on the stage, waiting for you." Daddy's information was meant for me, but his vengeful glare was aimed at my wide-eyed honey.

"Don't worry." I squeezed Jeremy's now cold and clammy hand. "Daddy's really a pussycat. Plus he so wouldn't do anything to injure his fragile relationship with your mother, the judge."

With Daddy leading the way and Jeremy close behind us, we snaked through the congested ballroom. I couldn't go two feet without some grateful guest trying to slow my progress. I signed three autographs and posed for five snapshots before Daddy realized I was being delayed behind his back. He shooed away my fans with threats of suing them for harassment, and we plunged forward.

In her chronic red chiffon, Veronica was waving from the bandstand. De and Kiki were beside her. And ranged across the stage behind them, in the shadow of Amber's humongous orange ball gown, were the rest of our Bronson Alcott and Grearly colleagues.

As I hurried up the stairs to join them, Veronica tapped the microphone. "Is this on?" she asked. The sound system, which had been cranked to a piercing pitch to accommodate the band, gave this ear-splitting screech.

"Duh, I guess so," Amber's magnified voice rang out.

Veronica laughed. A sound engineer rushed forward to adjust the mike. "Is everyone having fun so far?" the movie star asked, stepping to the edge of the stage.

"TOTALLY!" The youthful audience responded, matching the decibel level of the mike.

"Well, here are the people we have to thank for this extraordinary event." Veronica stepped back and, to another awesome burst of enthusiasm, indicated our crew.

"In particular, I'd like to introduce you to the three

young people who were instrumental in not just creating this fun-filled evening, but in saving this fabulous house . . . about which I intend to tell you much more shortly." Veronica stepped back and did this Vanna move, showing off me, Kiki, and De as though we were winning letters some contestant had just bought on *Wheel of Fortune*. And just like on *Wheel,* everyone started screaming again.

"For those of you who don't recognize one of today's most photographed young cover girls, this is Kiki Blunt." Veronica reached for the black-sheathed teen model's arm and tried to urge her forward. Kiki turned to De and me, trying to catch our hands and bring us with her. But we just gave her these supportive smiles and this little push forward, then applauded along with everyone else.

Veronica talked about the fashion show Kiki had put together. And then, as De and I exchanged these disappointed glances, the megastar looked down at Ronald Blunt, who was standing front row center, and asked if he'd like to join his daughter onstage.

De and I were all, Hello, when had the media-manipulating mogul ever turned down a sound bite? Blunt had like fifty publicity people working round the clock to keep his name and face in the news. The motor-mouthed builder never turned down a spotlit moment. He was probably in the *Guinness Book* for snagging more TV airtime than brush fires in Laurel Canyon. The man was a walking photo op. For sure, he'd steal Kiki's golden moment.

But Blunt shook his dark, stiffly moussed head.

"No thanks," he advised Veronica. "The kid totally eclipsed her old man on this one. It's Kiki's night."

De and I gave each other a limp Beverly Hills high-five as Kiki took her solo in the spotlight. "How moving is this moment?" My bud whispered as our co-chair tossed kisses to the crowd.

"Way. But not enough to trash your makeup," I advised, slipping my bud a tissue.

De was still daubing at her velvet hydro-light lash-enhancing mascara when Veronica called her name. She stepped forward, all radiant in blue satin and strappy slingbacks by Jimmy Choo. The ballroom and the stage behind us erupted in raucous applause and furious shouts of "You go, girl!"

Murray's proud voice rang out above the rest. "There go my shorty!" De's man bellowed.

"Straight up!" Sean backed the boy as my best bud stood stage center, her perfectly toned arms raised in triumph, her hazel eyes blinking back big, gloppy, purple-tinged tears.

And then before I knew it, Dionne and Kiki had seized my hands and were frantically propelling me forward. Whistles and screams and foot-stomping kudos rocked the ballroom. "And the person without whom none of this would be possible," Veronica was shouting into the mike, "Cher Horowitz."

I scanned the raving rooters arrayed before me. Miss Geist, who had first challenged us to take up the Llewellyn cause, was beaming at me while trying to scrape a caviar smear off her pale silk jacket. Mr. Hall, who had forced us to compose our complaint letters, was cheering me, too, joining the kids going, "Cher! Cher! Cher!" Arms over her head in a victory clench, there was Coach Diemer in her one good suit, which she'd evidently picked up at the reduced rack at Goodwill. Ruark and Maura were giving me these warm, fuzzy smiles, which is what the infatuation-stricken do to everyone all the time anyway. But even Josh was saluting me with a full-out thumbs-up. And of course, Daddy and my brutal babe, Jeremy, were both extremely kvelling.

"I like totally couldn't have done this without the aid and inspiration of so many people—" I began.

Suddenly, the sea of applauding humanity before me abruptly parted, its screams going from congratulatory to appalled.

"Oh, no," I heard De gasp. "It's Butta Boy and Mongo!" And these two humongous hams, these lumbering slabs of beef, a sharkskin-suited blubber syndicate, stomped down the center of the ballroom toward the stage.

"Murray!" De shrieked, hands on her ice blue, tulle-capped hips. "What are these people doing here?"

"I told you I was working on something big," the boy said sheepishly as the Grearly guys and other wrestling fans in the crowd began to recognize the notorious hulks and shout out their approval.

"Dudes, this is the coolest bash in recorded history," Ryder assured us.

"Like you'd know," Amber rebuked the boy.

But De, Kiki, and I looked out at the bedlam before us. Veronica had turned to Whitney, and after a moment the Hollywood divas had both furiously burst out laughing. The models, in their classic movie costumes, piled out onto the runway to catch a glimpse of the bulky hulks. Coach Diemer was screaming, "Mongo is the man!" And Ronald Blunt had grabbed a photographer and was having his picture taken with the grossly obese muscle men.

"How fun is this blowout?" Kiki asked, cracking up.

"Girlfriend," De told her, as the three of us hugged, "it's a totally Cher affair."

About the Author

H. B. Gilmour is the author of the best-selling novelizations *Clueless* and *Pretty in Pink*, as well as *Clueless™: Cher's Guide to . . . Whatever;* the Clueless™ novels *Achieving Personal Perfection, Friend or Faux, Baldwin from Another Planet, Cher and Cher Alike,* and *Romantically Correct; Clarissa Explains It All: Boys;* the well-reviewed young-adult novel *Ask Me If I Care;* and more than fifteen other books for adults and young people.